D0718960

AN
Enid Blyton
OMNIBUS

CRESSET
EDITIONS

This edition first published by Cresset Editions 1994
An imprint of the Random House Group
20 Vauxhall Bridge Road
London SW1V 2SA

First published in this collected edition 1994

All rights reserved. No part of the publication may be
reproduced, stored in a retrieval system, or
transmitted in any form or by any means, electronic,
mechanical, photocopying, recording or otherwise,
without the prior permission of the copyright owner.

The Yellow Fairy Book
Text © Enid Blyton 1936
Illustrations © Gunvor Edwards 1993

The First Green Goblin Book
Text © Darrell Waters Limited 1935
Illustrations © Paul Crompton 1992

The Second Green Goblin Book
Text © Darrell Waters Limited 1935
Illustrations © Paul Crompton 1993

The First Green Goblin Book and *The Second Green Goblin Book*
first published as The Green Goblin Book. *The Yellow Fairy Book*
first published as The Queer Adventure.

Enid Blyton's signature is a registered trademark
of Darrell Waters Limited

ISBN 0 09 181890 7

Random House UK Ltd Reg. No. 954009

Printed and bound in Great Britain by
Mackays of Chatham PLC, Chatham, Kent

CONTENTS

THE YELLOW FAIRY
BOOK

CHAPTER ONE

The Little
Princess Fenella

This is the story of a strange adventure. It happened to two children, Peter and Mary. They were twins and lived with their father and mother in a small cottage.

Their home was in a most exciting place, for their cottage was just outside the gates of Fairyland. Their mother sometimes did washing for the little folk, and she was allowed to go shopping in the little village inside the golden gates.

The children loved to go with her. At first the fairies had not been very pleased to see a boy and girl in their village beyond the gates, but they soon liked them very much.

'Come and have tea with me,' said Fairy Tiptap. 'I'll give you lemonade cakes, a kind you've never had before!'

'Come and see my big black cat,' said the pixie

Tippitty. 'He keeps house for me. Nobody can sweep or dust better than he can!'

But the greatest excitement of all was when Lady Rozabel came clattering along in her

coach one day, and saw Peter and Mary. She liked the look of them so much that she stopped her coach at once and leaned out of the window.

'Who are these children? I want companions for my little girl, the Princess Fenella, and I think perhaps they are just the right age to be with her,' she said.

Out of the window peeped the small Princess. She had curly golden hair, eyes like forget-me-nots, and the naughtiest smile that ever was seen.

'Mother!' she said, when she saw Peter and Mary. 'I like these children. I want them to play with me!'

'If they come, they will have to work with you, too,' said the Lady Rozabel. 'Perhaps you will do your lessons better then!'

Peter and Mary went to tea with Fenella, and the Lady Rozabel thought what good manners they had, and how kind they were to naughty little Fenella. That was the beginning of a grand time for the two children!

Fenella had wonderful toys and loved to share them with Peter and Mary. They shared lessons too, and Fenella worked much harder than usual because she didn't want to be beaten by her two new friends.

After lessons they played in the garden. It was a most exciting place. There was a magic swing, which if you shut your eyes, would swing you to anywhere you wanted to go – but it was dangerous to get off the swing until you were home again, because you might be left behind in some strange place!

There was a little river where they sailed boats, and paddled and bathed. There was a tiny house just big enough for the three children to get inside and play housekeeping. There was a very high tree from which, if they climbed to the top, they could actually see the towers of Giantland, very far away.

And there was the Magic Well. The children were not allowed to go near this.

'Remember, children, never go near the Magic Well,' Lady Rozabel told them over and over again. 'Something dreadful will happen if you do.'

Now one day Fenella lost her favourite ball. The three children hunted everywhere but they couldn't find it. Fenella flung herself down on the grass, and wailed loudly.

'What's the matter with the little lady!' suddenly said a shrill voice. The children looked round in surprise, and saw a small gnome stooping over a stick, his long beard reaching to the grass. He had bright green eyes that shone strangely.

'I've lost my ball and can't find it,' said the Little Princess, staring at the strange fellow.

'Well – go to the Magic Well and wish for it!' said the gnome. 'Don't you know that you have only to bend over the well and whisper your wish for it to come true?'

'Really!' said all the children, excited. 'Well – let's go!'

'I'll show you the way,' said the gnome, and he hobbled along in front of them. He took them to a small glade, a dim and silent place where no bird sang, and no rabbit peeped. Peter felt uneasy and wanted to go back, but Fenella shook her curly head at once.

'I'm going to wish!' she said. 'I'm *not* going back till I've wished for my ball!'

'Let Mary wish first, or me,' said Peter. 'Just to see if it's all right, you know.'

'Well, make haste then,' said Fenella.

Peter bent over the deep well. The water seemed a long way down. Cold air came up from it and he shivered. He knew what he wanted to wish. His mother was often ill – it would be lovely if she could always be well.

'I wish that my mother may never be ill again, but may always be well and strong,' he said firmly.

'That's a fine wish,' said Mary. 'Now *I'll* wish. I wish that my daddy will one day be rich and have a fine house!' she called down the well.

'That's a good idea too,' said Peter. 'Now, Fenella, wish for your ball.'

'No – first it is *my* turn,' said the gnome suddenly, in a strange voice. He pushed the children aside and leaned over the well. Peter was angry.

'No – it's Fenella's turn!' he said. 'How dare you be so rude to a princess!'

The gnome pushed Peter away roughly. Then he suddenly caught hold of Fenella and shouted loudly,

'I wish to be away, away, away!'

And, to the children's dreadful dismay, the gnome and Fenella vanished completely! Then there was a gurgling of water and the well vanished too! Nothing was left of it, not even a brick or a shining drop of water!

'Fenella's gone!' cried Peter, scared.

'Whatever are we to do?' said Mary, trembling. 'Call her, Peter.'

'Fenella! Fenella!' shouted Peter, looking all through the glade. But there was no one at all. Fenella had vanished with the gnome.

'I might have guessed he was up to mischief,' said Peter, miserably. 'He had such strange green eyes.'

'We'll have to tell the Lady Rozabel,' said Mary, tears running down her cheeks. So the two of them rushed to the palace with their bad news.

'Fenella's gone!' they cried. 'A gnome took her away, just by the Magic Well!'

At once there was a great upset. The gardens were searched from end to end. The well was hunted for, but, of course, it could not be found.

'You bad children!' raged Lord Rolland, Fenella's father. 'Weren't you told not to go near the well? Now the gnome Sly-One has got Fenella, and goodness knows what will happen. He may keep her prisoner – he may sell her for gold – he may even turn her into a black cat and keep her for a servant! I once turned him out of Fairyland and he vowed he would pay me out for that – now he has!'

'Go home!' said Lady Rozabel, weeping

bitterly. 'You should be beaten for letting Fenella go near the well. Go home – and never come back!'

The two children ran off at once, scared and miserable. Through the golden gates of Fairyland they went and back to their cottage home.

They found their mother ill in bed. Their father was tending her, dressed in his rough shepherd clothes.

'Our wishes didn't come true,' said Peter, sadly. 'Mother is ill instead of well – and our father is still a poor shepherd, and not a rich man.'

'Oh Mother!' cried Mary, 'a dreadful thing has happened!' She sank down by her mother's bed and told her everything.

'This is a terrible thing,' said her mother. 'The poor Lady Rozabel – and poor little Fenella! Why, oh why did you let her go near that well! There is only one thing to do – you must go and find the little Princess!'

CHAPTER TWO

The Beginning of the Adventure

Peter and Mary stared at their mother in surprise. 'But Mother! We don't know where she is!' said Peter.

'I think I can guess,' said his mother. 'She will be with the gnome Sly-One, of course, and he will have taken her to his own land.'

'Where's that?' asked Peter, eagerly.

'Well, when the Lord Rolland turned him out of Fairyland, he went to the Land of Story-tellers,' said his mother. 'A very good place for such a sly rascal, too! I'm sure that is where he has taken the little princess.'

'But how do we get there?' asked Mary. 'I've never even heard of such a land, Mother.'

'I can tell you,' said her father. 'You must first find your way to the Land of the Stupids. It's a great pity to have to go there — you may find

15

it difficult to get away. Then from there you must travel through Giantland.'

'Oh dear – I don't like that,' said their mother. 'Try not to be seen there, my dears. You never know what may happen if the giants catch sight of two little people like you.'

'After Giantland you will come to the Land of Storytellers,' said their father. 'When you get there you must find out where the gnome Sly-One lives, and see if you can somehow rescue the Princess.'

'It all sounds very difficult and rather frightening,' said Mary, afraid.

'Don't worry, Mary, *I'll* look after you,' said Peter, squeezing her arm. 'It will be a great adventure with something worth winning at the end. If we never come back at least we shall have tried to do something. The thing is – which is the way to the Land of the Stupids?'

'I can help you, I think,' said their father. 'I will take you to the Enchanted Wood. In the middle of it is an enormous tree, the Faraway Tree.'

'Whatever kind of tree is that?' said Mary in surprise.'

'It's a strange tree,' said her father. 'All kinds of little folk live in it. At the top is a great branch that pierces through the clouds. A little yellow ladder leads up from the branch – and at the top you will find a strange land.'

'A land – at the top of a *tree*!' cried Peter. 'What land?'

'Well, a new land comes every week,' said his father. 'Sometimes it may be the Land of Spells, sometimes the Land of Secrets, sometimes Toyland, sometimes the Land of Birthdays. And soon the Land of Stupids will be there.'

'Oh!' cried Peter. 'So if we climb the Faraway Tree we may get to the Land of Stupids quite easily. How do you know all this, Father?'

'I have a cousin who lives in the tree,' said his father. 'A little fellow called Moonface. I meet him sometimes, when I am watching my sheep, and he gives me the news of the Faraway Tree, and tells me about the strange lands that come there. We will set off now. If we delay you may miss the Land of Stupids.'

'Take some food with you,' said their mother. 'And look – take this too. It may be of some use. It is the only precious thing I have.'

She held out to Peter a small round box rather like a pill-box. Peter took it and opened it. Inside was some purple powder as fine as flour.

'What is it for?' asked the boy, in surprise.

'You must wait and see,' said his mother. 'If you do not use it, bring it back. My old granny, who was half a fairy, gave it to me. It is rare and very valuable. If the right time comes, you will use it – but not until.'

'Come,' said their father. 'We must hurry, or night will be on us. It is a long way to the Enchanted Wood.'

'Goodbye, dears,' said their mother. 'There's nothing much more I can say to you, except to tell you to be brave and kind.'

'We promise to be,' said the twins, and kissed their mother. 'Goodbye! We'll find the Princess and bring her back – we'll do our very best!'

Off they went with their father. He took them over the fields to a big hill, and down the other side. They walked through valleys, and passed many villages, and at last they came to the Enchanted Wood.

The Faraway Tree was right in the middle. When the children came to it they stared in surprise. It was so enormous! They looked up and up, and saw that its topmost branches reached the clouds.

A little squirrel in a red jersey came bounding up. 'Sir,' he said to the children's father, 'I am sure I have seen you before. You are Mr Moonface's cousin! Shall I take you up to his little house in the top of the tree?'

'Thank you,' said everyone, and followed

the squirrel as he bounded up the tree. The children were surprised and delighted as they climbed. There were little windows and doors in the tree, and how they wished they could peep in at the windows and knock at the doors!

But there was no time. They mustn't miss the Land of the Stupids! At last they came to the top of the tree, and saw a little door there, set in the round trunk. The squirrel knocked and it opened.

A little man with a round, shining face and

twinkling eyes looked out. 'Why – if it's not Cousin John the shepherd!' he said. 'And his two children. Come along in!'

'Well – we don't know if we've time to stop,' said the children's father. 'My two children want to go to the Land of Stupids, and I believe it's about time it came to the top of the Faraway Tree, isn't it?'

'Yes, it comes tomorrow,' said Moonface. 'So do come in and stay the night. How nice to see you all!'

They all went into Moonface's little round room inside the tree. The furniture was curved to fit round the inside of the trunk. In the middle was a big hole.

'Don't go near it unless you want to find yourself at the bottom of the tree!' said Moonface. 'That's my slippery-slip – a short cut to the foot of the tree. It goes round and round and down and down all through the tree.'

The children thought it sounded very exciting and longed to try it. But they didn't because they were tired, and they knew they would have to climb all the way up the tree again if they found themselves at the bottom!

Moonface gave them a lovely supper, and then the children curled up on a sofa and went to sleep. To think that the Land of Stupids would be there tomorrow! How very, very exciting!

Next morning Moonface woke them up. 'Hurry,' he said, 'I've got your breakfast waiting for you. The Land of Stupids is at the top of the tree – I've just been to look – it must have come in the night.'

They ate their breakfast quickly, and then followed Moonface out of his strange little house. The topmost bough of the tree reached up through a hole in the clouds.

'You go up there,' said Moonface, 'and then you come to a little yellow ladder. Climb it and you will find yourself in the Land of Stupids. Goodbye and good luck!'

'Goodbye, my dears,' said their father and gave them each a hug. 'I wish I could come with you, but somebody must look after your mother and the sheep. Goodbye!'

Up the bough climbed the two children and came to the yellow ladder. Up that they went – and suddenly their heads popped out through the cloud – and my goodness me, they found themselves in a sunny green field at the top of the tree. How very strange!

They stood there, gazing all round. In the distance was what looked like a village.

'That must be where the Stupids live!' said

Peter. 'Well, this is the first stage of our journey. We'll go and ask the way to Giantland, and from there we may be able to get to the Land of Storytellers. We're doing well!'

Off they went, and in ten minutes' time they came to the village. But dear me, *what* a village!'

CHAPTER THREE

In the Land of Stupids

The village was full of strangely-built houses. All of them were crooked and many of them seemed about to tumble down. Some had chimneys at the side instead of at the top. A great many had doors near the roof, which had to be reached by ladders.

'What stupid-looking houses!' said Peter. 'Did you ever see anything like them, Mary?'

'I never did!' said the little girl, staring round in astonishment. 'Look at *that* house, Peter! It hasn't any doors at all – only windows!'

'And that house opposite has only doors and no windows at all!' said Peter, beginning to laugh.

It certainly was a strange place – and the people were just as strange! The children soon met some of the Stupids. They were round, fat people, with great big heads and large, staring blue eyes.

'They look like grown-up babies!' said Mary, with a giggle.

They were dressed strangely. Their clothes were all right, but they didn't seem to know how to put them on. Nearly all of them had their coats on back to front, and their buttons were buttoned wrongly. One Stupid went by with a shoe on one foot and a boot on the other.

The children stared at him and could hardly wait to laugh until he had gone by.

'We've got to get to Giantland from here,' said Peter. 'Don't let's spend much time in this silly village, Mary. Let's ask how to get to Giantland, and go on.'

So they stopped the next Stupid and spoke to him. He was a funny-looking creature with a sailor hat on, but as he had it on side-to-front, the ribbon dangled over his nose and made him blink all the time.

'Good morning,' said Peter politely. 'Please could you tell us the way to Giantland?'

The Stupid stared at him and blinked quickly. He made no answer at all.

'Perhaps he's deaf,' said Mary. So she asked the question, this time in a very loud voice.

'PLEASE COULD YOU TELL US THE WAY TO GIANTLAND?'

'It's a long way, but you can get there if you start,' said the Stupid suddenly, as if it was a great effort to answer.

Peter thought that was a silly sort of answer.

'Yes, but which is the way?' he asked.

'Well, there's only one way and that's the right way,' said the Stupid, grinning.

'Of course!' said Peter impatiently. 'But which is the *right* way?'

25

The Stupid stared at him for a long time, blew the ribbon away from his nose and then scratched his head.

'Ah!' he said at last, very gravely. 'Ah!'

'Ah what?' said the children together, puzzled.

'Oh, just ah!' said the Stupid, and he grinned as if he had said something really very clever.

Peter pulled Mary away, scowling. 'Silly creature!' he grumbled. 'What does he mean with his stupid "Ahs!"? Can't he tell us the way without such a lot of blinking and talking?'

'He certainly was a Stupid!' said Mary, beginning to laugh, as she turned and saw the Stupid watching them, his ribbon dangling over his nose. 'We'll ask someone else. They can't all be as silly as that!'

They walked on down the twisted street. They came to a very crooked little house with two chimneys built in the side, very near the ground. Smoke was pouring out of them and streamed towards a clothes' line on which a small Stupid was putting clothes.

'Just look at that!' said Mary, stopping. 'Did you ever see anything sillier than someone putting out clean clothes where dirty smoke can spoil them!'

They stood and watched the small Stupid. She had a basket full of clean clothes, and these she hung higgledy-piggledy over the line, anyhow. A wind came and blew two of the clothes down to the grass. The Stupid picked them up, shook them and flung them over the line again.

'Why don't you *peg* them on?' called Mary, quite annoyed to see such silliness. She had often hung out the washing for her mother and knew just how it should be done.

'Why should I peg them on?' asked the little Stupid, staring at the children with round blue eyes. 'That would only make more work for me!'

'No, it wouldn't!' said Mary. 'You make far more work for yourself if you *don't* peg them on, because you have to keep picking them up when the wind blows them off – and besides, they will soon get dirty if they keep falling on the ground.'

'Oh, how clever of you!' said the Stupid, in delight. She ran indoors and brought out a box of brand-new pegs that had evidently never been used. She had no idea what to do with them, so Mary pushed open the crooked little gate and went into the garden. In a few minutes she had neatly and tightly pegged up all the clothes in a row, and then no matter how the wind blew, they could not fall.

The little Stupid watched her in admiration.

'Thank you,' she said. 'Thank you very much indeed. They won't fall down now. I never thought of that before. I suppose you couldn't tell me why my clothes always seem so dirty when I come to take them in? No matter how I wash them they always seem full of smuts when I take them indoors to iron.'

'Well, *I* can tell you the reason for that!' said Peter. He pointed to the chimneys that were puffing out black smoke on to the clothes. 'Just look where you've got your clothes' line – right beside those chimneys! The smoke puffs over them all the morning and fills them with smuts. I never saw such a silly place to put a clothes' line!'

The Stupid stared at him open-mouthed.

'You clever boy!' she said. 'You must come with me to the Head-Stupid. He will be so pleased to meet clever people like you.'

'Shall we go and see him?' Peter said to Mary. 'He would know the way to Giantland if anyone would.'

'Yes – let's go,' said Mary. So they let the little Stupid lead them down the street to a bigger house at the end. It was a little more sensibly built than the others, but seemed to have far too many doors. The little Stupid knocked on the biggest door and a voice called 'Come in!'

They opened the door and went in. Inside there was a big room with a large fire-place at one end. Over it a large Stupid was sitting, muffled up in coats and scarves.

'Are you cold?' cried Mary in surprise. 'It's such a lovely day outside!'

The house was full of draughts. The fire smoked badly and the children's eyes were soon smarting. The big Stupid looked at them solemnly.

'Of course I'm cold,' he said, in a grumbling sort of voice. 'So would you be if you lived in a house as draughty as this one! And this wretched fire! No matter what I do to it, it always smokes!'

'Well, why do you have so many doors?' asked Peter, looking round. He counted six doors leading into the one room. How ridiculous! 'No wonder you are always in a draught, and no wonder that your fire smokes, with six doors all round you! And badly fitting doors too!'

'Would that be the reason?' asked the big

Stupid in surprise. 'Dear me, I never thought of that! You must be very, very clever.'

'No, I'm not,' said Peter. 'I'm just an ordinary little boy, but I hope I've got some common sense. If you would have some of these doors taken away and the doorways built up, you would soon find that your room would be as warm as toast and your fire would stop smoking!'

'But it would be better still if you came out-of-doors on this lovely day and got warm in the sunshine!' said Mary.

The big Stupid looked at them with his large blue eyes and seemed to be thinking hard. Then he smiled and nodded. 'You are clever children,' he said. 'I would like your help in some difficulties that are puzzling me.'

'Well, *we* would like your help too,' said Peter. 'Do you know the way to Giantland?'

'Yes,' said the Stupid. 'Yes, I do. I have never been there, but I know the way.'

'How do we get there then?' asked Peter.

'If you'll help me, I'll help you,' said the Stupid, blinking his big staring eyes at them.

'All right. What do you want us to help you with?' asked Peter impatiently. He was getting rather tired of the Stupids.

'I am Head-Stupid and once a day my people come to me with complaints and grumbles,' said the Stupid. 'Perhaps you could tell them what to do?'

'Oh, yes, they could!' said the small Stupid, suddenly and eagerly. She had been standing in a corner, listening, and now she came forward. 'These clever children taught me how to stop the wind from blowing my washing away, and told me why it gets so smutty each week. They could help us a lot, Master!'

'Good,' said the Head-Stupid. 'Ring the bell, please, and tell the people to come round with their grumbles.

The small Stupid ran outside and the children heard her ringing a bell. The Head-Stupid got up and went outside. He sat down on a mat there and beckoned to the children to sit beside him.

Presently up the crooked streets came a crowd of the Stupids. They sat down in a ring round the Head and looked at him with their staring blue eyes. Then one got up and bowed.

'Master, my feet hurt me. What can I do? Shall I have to buy crutches?'

Peter and Mary looked at his feet and began to giggle. The silly creature had got his boots on the wrong feet! No wonder they hurt him!

'Take your boots off and put each one on the other foot!' called Peter. 'Then you will be able to walk comfortably!'

The Stupid unlaced his boots and did as he was told. Then he stood up and walked about. A smile spread over his broad face.

'My feet are healed!' he said. 'I can walk in comfort!'

'Well, don't put your boots on the wrong feet

again, stupid!' said Peter. 'Fancy not knowing your right foot from your left!'

'Master, I cannot see with my glasses,' said a fat little woman, whose shawl was round her waist instead of over her shoulders. She held out her glasses to the Head-Stupid. He gave them to Peter. He could see nothing wrong with them. He put them on and found that they magnified things very much. They were for someone very short-sighted.

He looked at the fat little Stupid. Her eyes looked back quite clearly. Surely she was not short-sighted!

'They are my grandfather's glasses,' she said to Peter. 'I like to wear them in memory of him, but my eyes go wrong when I do.'

Mary began to laugh. Fancy wearing glasses that belonged to someone else and expecting them to suit your own eyes!

'If you take the glass part out and look through the rims you will find that you can see perfectly!' she said, for she was quite sure, and so was Peter, that there was nothing wrong with the Stupid's eyes. The Head-Stupid at once took the glasses from Peter, smashed the glass part, took the splinters from the frame and gave the spectacles back to the woman.

She put them on and gave a cry of delight.

'I can see through my glasses now!' she cried joyfully, blinking through the glassless spectacles. 'My eyes are all right!'

Peter and Mary couldn't help laughing. Why wear the spectacles at all if she could see through them without any glass? But that never once came into the head of the fat little woman!

Then, to Peter's surprise, all the Stupids who were wearing glasses solemnly took them off, broke the glass and put on their spectacles once more – without any glass in them.

'Much better, much better!' they said gravely nodding to one another. The children stared in surprise. Were there ever such stupid people! They thought that *one* person's mistake must be everyone's!

'Please, Master, I can't reach my coat pockets no matter how I try!' said another Stupid, coming forward. The children looked at him. He was very plump, and as he had put on his coat back to front – and, of course, buttoned it all wrong – he found it was impossible to reach round to his pockets, which were now at the back instead of at the front.

'Take off your coat, put it on the other way, and you'll find you can reach your pockets,' said Peter at once.

The Stupid did so – and when he found that

he could then put his hands into all his pockets he was overjoyed. He pulled out all sorts of things and examined them carefully, as if he hadn't seen them for months – which, Peter thought, was quite likely, as it would never occur to him to look through the pockets when he had the coat off!

'Clever, very clever!' cried everyone admiringly.

One after another the Stupids asked their silly questions, which the children found easy to answer. When everyone had finished, Peter turned to the Head-Stupid.

35

'Now we've helped you as we said we would,' he said. 'Will you tell us the way to Giantland?'

'Well, it's dinner-time now,' said the big Stupid. 'Let's have something to eat.'

They went inside the smoky house and two little Stupids set a table. They set it very badly, the children thought, for they put the knives on the left-hand side and the forks on the right.

'Just as if we were all left-handed!' Mary whispered to Peter. The meal was served the wrong way round, too. The pudding came first, and then the meat and vegetables!

'Now it's time for a nap,' said the Head-Stupid, and he straightway lay down on his unmade bed and began to snore.

The children stared at him crossly. What a lot of time they were wasting! Why couldn't he have told them the way to Giantland before he went to sleep.

'Let's wake him up,' said Peter. So they dug him in the ribs and clapped him on the shoulder. But he simply turned over on his other side and snored even more loudly. Then Mary took a sponge that was, of all funny places, lying in the coal scuttle, filled it with water and squeezed it over the Stupid's face. Still he didn't wake!

'It's no good,' said Peter in disgust. 'I believe he's pretending to be asleep just so that he shan't tell us our way.'

The children did not get away from the Land of Stupids that day, for the Head-Stupid slept until six o'clock and then he wanted his supper. He kept putting the children off until they both became angry.

'You are very mean!' burst out Peter suddenly. 'We've kept our part of the bargain. Why don't you keep yours? If you *don't* know the way to Giantland why don't you say so?'

'But I *do* know it!' said the Head-Stupid annoyingly. 'And don't you speak to me like that, or I'll have you locked up!'

'Whatever for!' cried Mary indignantly. 'Can't we tell you if we think you're not playing fair? You great silly Stupid, I don't believe you know what it is to keep a promise!'

The Stupid clapped his hands five times and four more Stupids came in at once. They wore what was supposed to be policemen's uniform, but somehow it had got all wrong. Their helmets were on sideways and were so big that the children could only see the mouths of the Stupids. Their coats, as usual, were back to front, and their trousers far too short. Instead of heavy boots they wore fancy bedroom slippers with blue rosettes on, and this made Mary laugh loudly.

'Lock them up for the night,' said the Head-Stupid – and to the children's dismay they were marched off to a little round house that was a sort of police cell, for it had bars on its only window, and a great bolt on its one door.

'Well, they seem to know how to build a prison all right,' said Peter gloomily, looking through the bars. 'It's too bad, Mary. We shall never get away!'

'I expect they don't want us to go,' said Mary. 'We are much too useful to them! I'm sure they'd like to keep us here to answer all their silly questions and to put everything right for them, just as long as ever they could!'

Peter stared at Mary, and then he answered her in excitement.

'Mary, I do believe you're right! That's why they won't tell us what we want to know! They don't want us to go! We're too useful! They'll try to keep us here as long as they can!'

'Oh dear!' said Mary in dismay. 'How ever can we get away?'

'We can't, if they lock us up like this,' said Peter, trying to see if he could force out the bars on the window. 'They may be stupid in most things – but they are clever enough to know how to keep what they want!'

The children sat frowning together in the little cell. There was a mattress there and one chair. That was all. There was no way of escaping. Outside they could hear the tramp of their four guards.

Suddenly Peter smiled to himself. Mary saw him. 'What are you smiling for?' she asked.

'I've thought of a way to beat the Stupids, Mary!' said Peter. 'Listen!' He dropped his voice to a whisper, so that if any of the guards were listening they could not hear. 'Tomorrow we will be even stupider than the Stupids! We won't be able to answer their questions, or, if we do, we'll answer them so stupidly that the silly creatures will think we're no use to them, and let us go. See?'

'Oh, yes!' said Mary at once. 'That's a very good idea. If they think we're not so clever after all they won't bother to keep us! That's what we'll do, Peter – we'll be as stupid as they are!'

They fell asleep soon after that and did not wake until the morning. The four guards unbolted the door and marched them out. They had breakfast with the Head-Stupid, who asked them most politely how they had slept.

'How did I sleep? Well, I slept with my eyes closed, I think,' said Peter solemnly, with a very stupid expression on his face, which made Mary giggle. The Head-Stupid said nothing more. He gave Peter a scornful look and went on with his breakfast. It was just as funny a breakfast as the dinner had been. It began with marmalade and toast and went on to bacon and eggs, finishing up with porridge!

'I want you to come and help me with my people's complaints again,' said the Head-Stupid, when they had all finished.

'Certainly,' said Peter, taking the Head-Stupid's hat and putting it on back to front. He looked so silly that Mary couldn't help giggling. She wished she could think of something silly to do too, such as taking off her socks and wearing them on her hands, but it was too much trouble! The Head-Stupid probably wouldn't notice, anyway!

When the bell rang the Stupids all came round again with their complaints and their grumbles. But this time the children were most unhelpful!

'My clock won't go!' said one Stupid, holding up a big clock. Peter felt certain that the Stupid had forgotten to wind it up, but he didn't say so. He took the clock gravely, shook it, turned it upside down and then handed it back.

'No, it won't go,' he said, and would say no more. The Head-Stupid frowned at him, but Peter pretended not to notice.

'I can't do up this coat I've just made,' complained another Stupid. She held up her coat and Mary saw that she had made all the button holes and stitched all the buttons on the same side of the coat – so of course she couldn't do it up! Mary took the coat and pretended to try to button it. Then she shook her head and handed it back to the anxious Stupid.

'It won't do up,' said Mary, and that was all *she* would say!

They would tell the Stupids nothing that morning and the Head-Stupid became more and more impatient. At last he lost his temper.

'I thought you were clever!' he stormed. 'I thought you knew more than we did! You are even sillier than the silliest Stupid in the village. I don't know how you managed to deceive me yesterday!'

'We told you we weren't clever,' said Peter. 'We are just an ordinary boy and girl.'

'Well you're no use to *us*!' said the Head-Stupid. 'You'd better go!'

'That's just what we want to do!' said Peter. 'Which is the way to Giantland?'

41

'I shan't tell you!' said the Head-Stupid meanly. 'Find out for yourself.'

Peter and Mary stared at him in disgust. What a mean horrid person he was! 'Come on, Mary,' said Peter, taking her hand. 'We'll leave this foolish place. Its people are even too stupid to have any manners!'

He put his hat on straight and the two children walked away from the village. They had no idea which way to go, but they thought they might perhaps meet someone who could tell them. Soon they had left the crooked houses behind and were on a high road. There was no one in sight at all.

They walked on in the hot sun and presently they saw that the road forked into three ways. Which one ought they to take?

'There's a signpost, Peter!' cried Mary suddenly, pointing to a three-fingered post standing not far off. 'It's got names on it. It's sure to say which way Giantland is!'

They ran to it. The first arm, pointing to the right, said 'This way to Giantland'.

'Good!' said Peter. 'We'll go that way.' Then he stopped and stared at the next arm, pointing to the left. It said 'Take this road to Giantland'.

'That's strange,' said Mary, puzzled. 'They can't *both* go to the same place, surely!'

The third arm said 'To Giantland, this way'.

'Why, all the roads seem to lead to Giantland, Mary,' said Peter, more puzzled than ever.

'Well, maybe Giantland is so big that it stretches in all directions,' said Mary wisely. 'Let's take the middle road. We're almost sure to be right then. If Giantland lies to the right *and* the left, there must be some in the middle too!'

'You're quite right!' said Peter. So they took the middle road, wondering very much what the land of Giants would be like.

CHAPTER FOUR

Among the Giants

The two children walked on for some time, and then coming behind them, they heard a noise like rolling thunder. They turned round in surprise – and saw a curious sight. The noise was made by the wheels of a most enormous cart, drawn by a horse as big as an elephant!

'Goodness!' cried Peter, pulling Mary to one side. 'Look at that! We must certainly be on the road to Giantland because there is a giant horse and cart.'

'And a giant driving them!' said Mary, peeping out from the bush in which she was hiding. The giant was humming a song as he passed by, and the sound was like the throbbing of an aeroplane. The children gazed at him in awe, for he was simply enormous. His eyes were as big as saucers, and his thick hair hung round his great head like ropes.

'I hope the giants don't see us as we go through their land,' said Peter, rather uneasily, when the horse and cart had thundered past. 'It wouldn't do to be caught by them, Mary. The best thing we can do is to keep to the side of the road among the bushes and hide whenever we see anyone coming. When we get to a village or a town we had better hide until night and then creep through it when it is dark.'

'That's a good idea,' said Mary. 'If the giants see us they will think we are dwarfs, we shall seem so tiny to them! We had far better keep out of their way. We shall come to another signpost sooner or later, and that will tell us the way to the Land of Storytellers – and then, hurrah! We'll soon find Fenella and get her home again!'

They felt happy as they walked on their way once more. It didn't seem very difficult to get through Giantland and then on to the place where Fenella was. They skipped along, until Peter noticed something strange.

'Look, Mary!' he said suddenly, stopping and pointing to the grass and the bushes they were passing. 'Do you notice how the grass seems to be getting taller and taller? And look at the trees! They are stretching up to the sky and their trunks are nearly as thick as the trunk of that big Faraway Tree we climbed in the Enchanted Wood.'

Sure enough it was true. The grasses were soon taller than the children, and the bushes seemed like young woods!

'It's *really* Giantland now!' said Mary. We shall find it very easy to hide, Peter. No giant will see us in this tall grass!'

They kept among the grass as much as they could. But not only the grass was giant-like; the insects were too! A large brown thing, with ugly-looking pincers at its tail-end, suddenly hurried by, nearly knocking Mary over.

'What was that?' she said to Peter, going quite pale. 'Was it a sort of dragon?'

'No,' said Peter, laughing. 'It was only a giant earwig! And look, whatever's that?'

It was a monstrous ladybird, her spotted back gleaming like a mirror, it was so bright. As she drew near to the children she stopped in alarm. She unfolded some gauzy wings from underneath her spotted back, spread them and flew away with a little buzzing noise.

'There she goes!' said Peter. 'A ladybird almost as big as a puppy!'

They went on, Peter keeping a sharp lookout for other creatures. They saw a great spider, its eight legs covered with thick hairs, looking at them from eight eyes set on its forehead. It did look strange and ugly. Peter was half-afraid it might think they were insects to be eaten, and he hurried Mary on as quickly as he could. They had to look out for webs, too, for Peter thought it would be a difficult thing to get out of a sticky web once they had blundered into it.

Soon they heard a crashing noise, and the children crouched down behind a tall buttercup, whose golden head waved high above them. An animal as big as a donkey came bounding through the grass. It was an enormous rabbit, its big ears twitching as it stopped just by the children listening.

After some while the children came to a village. The houses all seemed as big as castles, so that to them the village seemed a vast town. Great carts thundered by, and enormous dogs sniffed about. Peter was afraid a dog might smell them out, and he looked round for a hiding-place.

He saw a hole not far off and took Mary to it. It was as big as a small tunnel. They squeezed down it and not far down found a kind of room hollowed out, lined with moss and leaves. It was quite cosy, but smelt rather musty.

'Does it belong to anyone, do you think?' said Mary.

'I shouldn't think so,' said Peter.

But it did! For suddenly there came a smooth, gliding sound and down the hole came a large round worm, soft and slimy! It had no eyes and could not see that there was anyone in its hole. It coiled itself round the children, and, when they struggled and shouted, let go in alarm. It shot up the hole again and disappeared.

'What a shock it got, poor thing!' said Mary.

'What a shock *we* got, too!' said Peter. 'We had better go, Mary. The worm might have

48

gone to get his friends to turn us out, and as they are as big as pythons it wouldn't be very pleasant. Come on!'

So out of the hole they crept, and went to look for another hiding place. Soon something strange happened. Great blobs of water bigger than dinner plates fell round them! One hit Peter on the head and knocked him over.

'Whatever is it!' he cried, shaking the water from him.

'It's raining!' said Mary. 'Giant rain! How strange! Come under this big thistle, Peter, till it stops.'

The thistle was a tall, prickly plant with its spines as long as spears. The children had to be careful not to get pricked or cut. They crouched under the broad thistle leaves and heard the raindrops falling around them thickly, and soon, to the children's great dismay, a little stream of water appeared behind the thistle.

'Oh my, I hope a puddle isn't going to come just here!' groaned Peter. The water spread around them. It was most annoying. If only they had chosen another plant to shelter under they could have climbed up its stem and sat on a leaf. But the thistle was set with such long sharp prickles that it was impossible to climb.

Just as the puddle was closing round the

children's feet a large white thing came sailing by. Peter and Mary stared at it.

'It's an enormous paper boat!' cried Mary, in surprise. 'Some giant boy or girl must have made it and set it sailing in the rain puddles. It's big enough for us to get into, Peter. Shall we stop it and climb inside?'

'Yes,' said Peter. 'The rain is stopping now, so we shan't get very wet if we sail off in the boat. Come on!'

He caught hold of the paper side of the boat and held it still whilst Mary stepped into it. Then Peter got in too. The boat swung round the prickly thistle and then rushed off down the stream of water, which was now as large as a river. The children clung to the paper middle of the boat. Along they went, now rushing to one side and now to another.

'Peter! I believe this boat is taking us to the village!' said Mary, in alarm.

'We'd better get out then,' said Peter. But by now the boat was going along far too fast. Sometimes it spun round and round and made the children giddy. They wished they had never climbed into it!

Suddenly the stream of water ran under a sort of bridge and came out into the gutter of a roadway! Peter and Mary stared in horror. They

were in the village where the giants lived, just the place they had been trying to keep away from whilst it was daylight! Now here they were, tearing along the gutter in a paper boat for all the giants to see! It was dreadful!

One or two giants were walking down the wide street, holding great umbrellas up to keep off the few drops of rain still falling. Nobody noticed the children at first – and then a little giant-girl saw them and shouted in excitement.

'Look! Look! Two little dolls in a boat!'

The giant-mother looked. The giant-girl ran to the gutter and picked up the boat, with Peter and Mary still in it. She picked them up so carelessly that Mary nearly fell out.

'Be careful!' yelled Peter, clutching hold of Mary's arm and just saving her in time. 'Be careful, giant-girl! You'll make us fall!'

The girl was so astonished to hear Peter's voice that she very nearly dropped the boat.

'Mother! They are not dolls, they are real!' she cried, in surprise.

'Well I never!' boomed the mother-giant, in amazement. 'Two little mannikins! Wherever could they have come from? We'll take them home, Grizel.'

'Put them in your market-bag, Mother,' said Grizel, the giant-girl. So into the mother's net-bag went Peter and Mary, among potatoes, cakes and a large cabbage whose thick leaves felt like leather.

They were carried in the bag for a long way. Peter found himself squashed against a delicious chocolate cake. As he was very hungry he thought he might as well make a meal whilst he had the chance. So he whispered to Mary, who was sitting in a cabbage leaf, and the two children took big handfuls of the cake and ate it.

At last they were taken into a great house and the giant-girl emptied them out of the bag.

'They are really alive,' said the mother-giant.

'Take them up to your nursery, Grizel. You will like them better than your dolls.'

So up to the nursery went Grizel, carrying Mary and Peter, one in each hand. She held them rather tightly so that they could hardly breathe, but at least they were not afraid of falling.

Grizel shut the door and set the children on the floor. There were enormous toys all round, all of them bigger than the children. In the corner stood a doll's house, not quite as big as a small, ordinary house would be to us. A large rocking-horse towered above the children and balls as high as an ordinary room were here and there. It was all rather frightening.

'Now I'm going to have a lovely game with you!' said Grizel, in delight. 'I'm going to play at being the old woman who lived in the shoe, and you shall be my children. I shall cook you some broth without any bread, and then I shall whip you soundly and put you to bed!'

Peter and Mary listed in horror. Good gracious, a smack from Grizel's huge hand would knock them flat. What an unpleasant child she must be!

Grizel got out a cooking-stove, a toy one to her, but as big as a real one to the children. She poured some water into a saucepan, scraped into it a bit of carrot, a speck of onion and a morsel of turnip, and then set them on the stove to cook.

'Goodness! Is that the broth!' said Peter to Mary. 'I jolly well won't eat it!'

Grizel took two small chairs out of her doll's house and sat the children down firmly on them. Peter was cross and jumped up again. *He* wasn't going to be sat down and stood up like a doll!

'Oh, naughty, naughty!' said Grizel. She tapped him with her finger and Peter shouted in pain, for the big girl's finger was as large as a log of wood, and bruised his shoulder dreadfully. He sat down again at once. It was no use offending a giant, even if she was only a small one!

Grizel took out a doll's table and set it before the children. She laid out small knives and forks and two dishes. By this time the broth was cooking, so she ladled some out of the saucepan into their dishes. It was steaming hot.

'There you are, children,' she said. 'Eat up your broth.'

Neither Peter nor Mary took up their spoons, for they could see the broth was too hot. Grizel picked up a spoon, filled it with the hot broth and tried to make Mary drink it. It burnt

Mary's mouth and she shouted in pain. Up jumped Peter in a rage and knocked over the dish of broth. It fell on to the giant-girl's foot and scalded her. She danced round, crying.

'Well, you shouldn't make Mary drink something that's too hot!' shouted Peter. 'It serves you right!'

But that was a silly thing to say to hot-tempered Grizel. She picked Peter up, slapped him hard, so that all the breath was forced out of him, and then took him to the doll's house. She opened the front of it, and put him into a small bed there.

'You *deserve* to be smacked soundly and put to bed!' scolded the giant-girl. She went back to Mary, slapped her too, and put her into another bed, just by Peter. Then she slammed shut the big front of the doll's house and left them.

Mary was crying. Peter, feeling all his bones to make sure that the rough giant-girl hadn't broken any, sat up in his bed.

'Are you hurt, Mary?' he called anxiously.

'No, only bruised where that great rough girl slapped me,' wept Mary. 'Oh, Peter, isn't this a horrible adventure? Oh, whatever are we going to do?'

Peter got out of bed and went to the window of the doll's house. He looked out.

'I don't know,' he said gloomily. 'The nursery door is shut and we shall never be able to climb up as high as the window.'

Just then the nursery door was flung open and in danced Grizel, her steps as loud as thunder. She went to the doll's house and peeped in at the window.

'Mother's letting me have a party this afternoon to show you off!' she called. 'All my friends are coming and we'll play lovely games

with you! You'll be like real, live dolls! I'll come
and get you ready in an hour's time. Some of my
doll's best clothes will fit you nicely.'

She danced out again, banging the door
behind her. She really was a very noisy person
indeed. Peter had fled back to bed as soon as he
had heard her coming. He didn't want to be
slapped again!

'Oh, Mary, did you hear what she said?' he
groaned. 'A party to show us off! That means
we'll be picked up and handled and squeezed
and squashed by lots more giant children like
Grizel. What in the world can we do?'

'Well, Peter, can't we hide somewhere?' said
Mary, getting out of bed. 'Grizel won't be
coming back for an hour. That's a long time.
Surely we can find somewhere in this big
nursery where we can hide safely till it's
night.'

'Yes, we'll hide!' said Peter. He jumped out
of the doll's bed once more and he and Mary
went down the little doll's house stairs together.
They opened the front door and looked out.
Where would be the best place to hide?

'There's a space under the toy cupboard.
Shall we hide there?' said Mary. But Peter
shook his head.

'No,' he said. 'They'd be sure to look there.

We must hide in some place where they'll never dream of looking.'

They began to hunt round. Should they hide in the box of bricks? No, that was much too dangerous. They might be tipped out with the bricks. What about in the coal-scuttle? No, it was very dirty, and besides, they might be put on the fire with the coal.

'Shall we get into one of the trucks belonging to the toy train?' said Peter. 'It's quite big enough to take us. We should be safe there.'

'*I* don't think we should,' said Mary. 'Grizel would look there, I'm sure. What about squeezing under the carpet, Peter?'

'That's silly,' said Peter, at once. 'We might be trodden on.'

The children looked round in despair. Wherever *could* they hide? They had already spent quite half-an-hour hunting here and there. And then a sound startled them dreadfully. It was a very loud voice indeed, crying 'Cuckoo! Cuckoo! Cuckoo!'

Mary clutched hold of Peter and looked round for the voice. Did it belong to another giant?

Then Peter pointed upwards and began to laugh.

'Look! It's a cuckoo clock!' he said. 'It's like

the one we've got at home. The cuckoo comes out of that little door at the top to call the hour.'

Mary stared up at it – and then a great idea came to her.

'Peter! Why shouldn't we hide in the little room where the cuckoo lives, at the top of the clock? No one would ever find us there!'

Peter shouted with delight.

'Good for you, Mary! The best idea you've ever thought of! Look, the clock has long winding-up chains reaching right to the floor, just as our clock at home has. We can easily climb up by putting our feet into the links of the chain.'

They ran to the chains that hung from the giant cuckoo clock. They could easily put their feet into the links. Up they went, the chains swaying as they climbed. It was a long climb, and the children's arms ached long before they reached the clock.

The clock was carved with leaves and birds. Peter and Mary swung themselves up on to a wooden leaf and climbed round the clock-face until they reached the little door at the top of the clock, behind which the cuckoo lived. Peter tried to open the door, but he couldn't.

'We'll wait until the cuckoo comes out next time and then slip in,' said Peter.

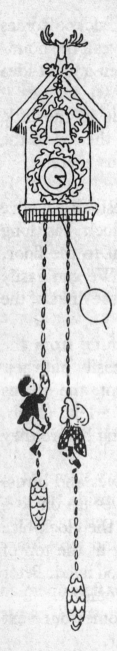

'But the next time it cuckoos it will be half-past three, and by that time Grizel will be here looking for us,' whispered Mary.

'Oh, goodness, I forgot that!' said Peter in dismay. He tugged at the door – but it would *not* open!

'We must crouch behind a leaf and hope that Grizel won't think of looking up here,' he said at last. So he and Mary squeezed themselves behind a carved leaf and waited. It was not very long before the nursery door flew open once more and in rushed the giant-girl. She went to the doll's house and opened the front of it.

'Come along, you little live dolls!' she called. 'It's time you were dressed for my party!'

Then she saw that they were not there! She gave a cry of rage and tumbled all the furniture of the little house out on to the floor, looking for them.

Then she jumped to her feet and shouted 'Mother! Mother! Those dolls have gone! Come and help me look for them! They must be hiding!'

Into the room came the giant-mother, dressed in her best. She and Grizel began to hunt round for the children. Peter and Mary trembled to see them.

'Just wait till I find them!' grumbled Grizel angrily. 'I'll give them such a smacking!'

'Is the cuckoo going to call the half-hour soon?' whispered Mary to Peter. 'We mustn't miss it, Peter.'

'We shall hear a whirring noise when it is going to come out and cuckoo,' whispered back Peter. 'Cheer up, Mary.'

They waited anxiously for the whirring noise. They were dreadfully afraid that the giants would look up and see them very soon. At last they heard the whirring noise inside the clock that meant that the cuckoo was getting ready to come out. Peter reached over and took Mary's hand.

Whizz! The little wooden door flew open, and out came the cuckoo, flapping small painted wings.

'Cuckoo!' the children heard.

At once Mary and Peter slipped in at the open door. The cuckoo jerked back and the door slammed shut. They were in the little room belonging to the cuckoo in the clock!

CHAPTER FIVE

Inside the
Cuckoo Clock

It was very dark there at first. Outside, the children could hear Grizel and her mother getting crosser and crosser.

'They're not under the cupboard!'

'They're not in the brick box!'

'They're not in any of the train trucks!'

'Where *can* they be? Bother them! It's too bad! I can hear our guests arriving downstairs, and now there are no wonderful live dolls to show them!'

'Have they climbed up behind any of the pictures?'

Then the children heard all the pictures being slightly turned, and they were glad to think that they had slipped inside the cuckoo-clock before the giants had thought of looking upwards. They might easily have been seen on the clock, whilst they were waiting for the cuckoo.

63

Gradually they began to be able to see what the inside of the cuckoo's little room was like – and then, what an enormous surprise they got!

It was a proper little room. There was a round table in the middle with a blue check cloth on it. There were chairs about and a shining cupboard in one corner. There was a tiny fire at the back of the room with a small kettle boiling away merrily – and sitting by it in a rocking chair was – the cuckoo!

At first the children thought the cuckoo was an old woman, sitting there knitting – but no, it was most certainly the cuckoo! She had a red shawl thrown over her shoulders, and she had slipped her feet into a pair of old slippers. There she sat, with spectacles on her nose, knitting away for dear life!

The children stared and stared. They didn't know what to say or do. This was the most surprising thing they had ever seen!

Presently the cuckoo lifted her head and looked at them twinklingly over her spectacles.

'Have you quite finished looking at me?' she asked, in a soft, cuckooing sort of voice. 'Am I such a surprise? Well, I can assure you that you are every bit as much of a surprise to *me*!' This is the first time I've ever had any visitors since I came here. It is most exciting.'

'We didn't know – we really didn't know you were properly alive and lived in a little room like this,' said Mary, finding her voice at last. 'We just thought we'd come and hide in the clock.'

'And a very good idea too,' said the cuckoo, knitting away steadily. 'Nobody would think of looking for you here. You are quite safe. I heard those giants looking for you down there. I'm glad Grizel didn't find you. She's a careless, spiteful creature. She often forgets to wind up this clock and then I can't go out of my door for days.'

'Do you mind us hiding here?' asked Peter.

'Not a bit,' said the cuckoo. 'I tell you I'm delighted to have someone to talk to. I do get so lonely up here in my little room. What about a bite of tea, now? Are you hungry?'

'Very,' said Peter, at once. 'Our dinner was only some chocolate cake in the giant's marketing-bag.'

'Can I help you?' asked Mary politely.

'Well that would be most kind of you,' said the cuckoo. 'My legs are rather bad today and I'd be glad to have someone waiting on me for a change. All the tea-things are in that cupboard over there. You can make the tea, and the boy can make us some toast. There are some sausages in the cupboard. We'll fry those too.'

'Will the giants hear us talking up here?' asked Mary anxiously.

'Bless you, no!' said the cuckoo comfortably. 'They don't know anything about my snug little room here. I heard it was to let years ago and came here, and here I've been ever since, with never a soul to peep in at me or say how do you do! So long as I cuckoo every half-hour and every hour that's all the giants care about!'

Soon the children were busy over the tea. Mary set the little table neatly, and Peter made a pile of toast. Then, whilst he fried the sausages – and dear me, *how* good they smelt – the little girl made the tea.

'It's all ready, Mistress Cuckoo!' she said.

The cuckoo brought her rocking-chair to the table and began to pour out the tea. Then she served the sausages, and the children ate them hungrily.

'This is a great treat for me,' said the kindly cuckoo, beaming at the children down her long beak. 'I do enjoy company and it's years since I had any. Now where did I put my best strawberry jam and those shortbread biscuits I've been saving up?' She got up and went to the cupboard. She found a large jar and a big tin.

Just as she was about to put them on the table the children were most astonished to see her turn herself about and rush swiftly to the door. She pushed it open and went out.

'Where's she gone?' asked Mary, in alarm. 'She isn't going to tell the giants about us, is she?'

'Cuckoo! Cuckoo! Cuckoo! Cuckoo!' called the cuckoo, in her loud, clear voice. Then she came back with a rush, slammed the door and put the jar and the tin on the table. She sank down on her chair and began to laugh.

'Oh my, oh my!' she said. 'Do you know, I almost forgot to cuckoo the hour! As it was I was two minutes late! Fancy that! And I went to the door carrying my tin and my jar of jam, and with my red shawl on! Whatever would the giants have thought if they had seen me? I really don't know! They would have taken the clock down at once and looked inside my room, there's no doubt!'

'Then we've had quite an escape,' said Peter, rather alarmed. 'We won't let you forget to cuckoo at the half-hour, Mistress Cuckoo!'

'No, please don't,' said the cuckoo, putting out some delicious-looking strawberry jam into a flowered china dish. 'I've never forgotten before. It was just the excitement of having visitors that made me forget. Now do have some jam with your buttered toast!'

The children ate an enormous tea. The jam was lovely, and the shortbread biscuits melted away in their mouths. Peter kept looking at his watch as the time went on.

'It's almost the half-hour, Mistress Cuckoo!' he said suddenly. At once the cuckoo got up, threw off her shawl and her slippers and went to open the door. She cuckooed loudly once and came back again.

'The nursery is full of giant children,' she said. 'It's the party going on, I expect. Can you hear the noise?'

The children listened. The cuckoo's room was high up and quiet, but they could quite well hear the loud shouts and heavy footfalls of the children below. They trembled to think that they might have been down there with them, being handled and squeezed.

'Don't look so frightened!' said the cuckoo, now quite comfortable again in her shawl and slippers. 'You're safe here. I wish you'd live with me always, I do like you so much.'

'We'd love to stay with you for a long time,' said Mary, smiling at the kindly cuckoo. 'But we are trying to rescue someone who has been captured by a wicked gnome, and we mustn't stay too long. Peter, you tell Mistress Cuckoo all about it.'

'We'd better clear away and wash up first,' said Peter, looking at the littered table. So the children set to work, much to the delight of the cuckoo, who had never been waited on before. They soon cleared the table and washed up in a little sink that was neatly hidden by a small red curtain. They put away all the things and then went to sit down by the fire. The cuckoo was rocking herself busily, still knitting.

'Now tell me all about yourselves,' she said cosily. 'You can't possibly go tonight, so take your time about it. I am so enjoying having you both!'

Peter told the cuckoo all his story, from the dreadful moment when Fenella disappeared to the time when he and Mary had climbed up the clock-chains. The cuckoo nodded her head and said 'Dear, dear!' now and then.

'Well!' she said, when Peter had finished, 'I do think you are two dear, brave children to set out on such a journey, and I hope you'll find Fenella. I do, indeed!'

'Do you know the best way to get from here to the Land of Storytellers?' asked Peter. 'Is it a very long way?'

'Well,' said the cuckoo, putting down her knitting, 'it *is* rather a long way. You see, Giantland is so big that it stretches for miles and miles and miles. I really don't know how you could walk through it without being seen a hundred times by the giants.'

'Oh, dear!' said Peter, in dismay, 'I don't want to be caught by giants again! Once is quite enough!'

'I should think so!' said the cuckoo.

'I suppose there's no way of *flying* over Giantland is there?' asked Mary. 'That would be so much better than walking all the way through it!'

'No – there's no aeroplane or anything,' said the cuckoo thoughtfully. 'I don't see *how* you could fly over – unless – unless –'

'Unless what?' cried the children excitedly.

'Well – unless *I* took you on my back and flew over Giantland!' said the cuckoo slowly.

The children stared at her.

'But *would* you?' asked Peter eagerly.

'I don't see why I shouldn't,' said the cuckoo, taking off her glasses and looking at the children. 'I used to be able to fly very well indeed. I shall have to practise a bit tonight, when the giants are all in bed. I could take a few turns round the nursery and see if my wings are

71

as strong as they used to be. Oh, I could fly very swiftly and well when I was younger!'

Mary jumped up and hugged the cuckoo till she gasped for breath and begged for mercy.

'You're a perfect dear to help us like this!' said Mary. 'Oh, how lovely it would be if we could miss out the rest of Giantland by flying right over it! I don't like the giants one bit.'

'Well, now, we can't do anything about it just yet,' said the cuckoo, rolling up her knitting and putting it into a black bag. 'What about a game of Snap? It's ages since I had a good game with anyone!'

'Oh let's!' cried the children. So the cuckoo got out a pack of curious snap-cards, all with giant-families on them, and they sat round the table and played until they were tired. Every half-hour the cuckoo had to get up and rush to the door to cuckoo, and once she took her snap-cards with her, she was in such a hurry. How they all laughed when she came back, looking flustered and hot!

'Do you know, I nearly called "Snap!" instead of "Cuckoo!" ' she said to the children. 'Whatever would the giants have thought?'

That made the children laugh even more. They had a lovely game until the cuckoo said it was time to stop and have supper. Mary and

Peter put her in her rocking-chair again and said they would manage supper.

'There is a jam-tart in the cupboard, and you'll find some cream in a blue jug!' said the cuckoo, getting out her knitting again. 'Make a jug of hot cocoa, and that will suit us all nicely!'

They had supper all together, joking and laughing. There was gooseberry jam in the tart, and plenty of sugar in the cocoa. It was great fun. After that the children cleared away and washed up. Then Mary yawned.

'Aha, it's bedtime for you!' said the cuckoo.

'Oh, no, do let me see you fly round the nursery!' begged Mary.

'Very well,' said the cuckoo. 'I'll just go and peep out to see if everything is safe.'

She went to her little door and pushed it open. The nursery was dark except for some light that came into it from the landing outside, where a big lamp burned.

'It's quite safe, I think,' said the cuckoo, peering out. She took off her shawl, which was wrapped round her wings and prevented her from spreading them properly. Peter and Mary went to the door and watched.

The cuckoo spread her wings and launched herself into the air. Round and round the nursery she went, flapping her wings. At last she came back quite delighted.

'My wings are even stronger because of the long rest I've had!' she said, pleased. 'I shall be able to carry you both very easily. Just half a minute!'

She turned to the nursery and cuckooed loudly ten times. It was ten o'clock!

'Now,' she said briskly, wrapping herself up in her shawl again and slamming the door. 'Now, it's time for bed! We must all get to sleep quickly, because my plan is that we set out at dawn, when all the giants are still asleep. With luck we should reach the land of Storytellers about eight o'clock, and I can be back in my clock before lunchtime. Perhaps no one will notice I am not cuckooing. Very often the giants are out all the morning shopping.'

The children were happy and very sleepy. Mary could hardly keep her eyes open.

'Where shall we sleep?' asked Peter, looking all round. He could not see a bed anywhere.

The cuckoo went to the wall and pressed a little knob. A panel slid aside and the cuckoo pulled out a neat little bed, complete with blankets and pillows.

'You have to hide things away when your room is as small as mine!' she said. 'Now there's just room for the two of you there. Undress and get in quickly, or you'll fall asleep where you're standing!'

'But where will *you* sleep?' asked Mary.

'In my rocking-chair,' said the cuckoo. 'I often take a nap there. I've got to be out of my door, cuckooing every half-hour, so my nights are never very peaceful. Now hurry up, both of you!'

Soon the children were tucked up in the small, but very soft and comfortable bed. They closed their eyes and fell fast asleep in two minutes! The cuckoo sat down in her rocking chair and took up her knitting. She was very happy. It was such a treat to have two cheerful, friendly visitors. She would remember this day for years and years!

At dawn she awakened the sleeping children. 'Time to be off!' she said. 'I've made some hot coffee for us, and there's some bacon and eggs cooking. They will be ready by the time you are dressed!'

The children smelt the good smell of frying bacon and hot coffee. They dressed quickly and were soon sitting down at the little round table enjoying their breakfast.

'There's not a soul awake in the house!' said the cuckoo, drinking her coffee. 'Not a soul!

We shall be able to fly off without anyone seeing us!

'What's that funny noise?' asked Mary, listening to a strange throbbing noise that rose and fell all the time.

'Oh, that's just the giants snoring,' said the cuckoo. 'They all do that. Now what about some marmalade with your toast, Peter?'

They all made a good breakfast and then the cuckoo gave some apples and chocolate to the children to take with them. She took off her shawl and gave it to Mary.

'I can't fly with it on,' she said. 'But you'd better use it as a rug to cover yourselves when you're on my back. The morning air is chilly. I shall keep my slippers on. I do have such dreadful chilblains if I don't. Now are we ready?' The children took a last look round the dear little room where they had been so kindly treated. Then they climbed on to the cuckoo's broad back and wrapped the red shawl round them. The cuckoo opened the door, told them to hold tight, and spread her wings.

Off they went into the air, circling round the nursery! The window was a little bit open at the top and the cuckoo flapped neatly through the crack and out into the cold morning air. The sun was just rising, and everything was touched with gold.

'Isn't this fun?' shouted Peter to Mary. 'Weren't we lucky to find such a kind friend?'

Mary cuddled herself into the shawl, for the morning was certainly cold. She smiled at Peter, and then looked down at Giantland. It was a strange place in the early sunlight. The houses towered up like enormous castles. The windows seemed endless, and shone brilliantly in the sun. The streets were very wide, and the cats that lay about here and there were as big as donkeys.

On and on flew the cuckoo, flapping her strong wings. For hour after hour she flew, and the children grew a little sleepy again, for they had not had a very long night. Mary yawned. The cuckoo heard her and turned her head.

'Why don't you try to get a nap?' she called in her soft, cuckooing voice. 'You will be quite safe on my back if you tuck your feet well into the fold of my wings.'

So for some while the children slept, their feet tucked into the warm folds of the cuckoo's wings, and their hands clinging to her neck-feathers. The sun rose higher and beat down warmly. Mary suddenly awoke, feeling far too hot.

She sat up and took off the shawl. Then she awoke Peter in excitement.

'Peter! I do believe we are out of Giantland now! Look down! The houses are no longer big.'

They looked down. It was quite true. They had passed right over Giantland and were now in another land. They called to the cuckoo.

'Yes!' she said, 'we are over the Land of Storytellers now. I'm taking you to the market-place as you will no doubt find plenty of people there to ask about the gnome Sly-One. We shall be there in two minutes.'

In a short time the cuckoo flew down to a crowded market-place, where gnomes of all kinds bought and sold, chattering and calling at the tops of their hoarse voices.

The children jumped off the cuckoo's back. 'Thank you ever and ever so much!' they said earnestly. 'You *have* been good to us!'

'Not at all, not at all!' said the cuckoo. 'I've been delighted to have you. Now I must say goodbye and get back quickly or the giants will miss me.'

The children felt sad at parting with such a good friend. Mary kissed the cuckoo on her beak and tucked her red shawl under her wing for her to take back. The cuckoo's eyes were full of tears, for she had liked the two children very much indeed.

'Goodbye, my dears, goodbye,' she said. 'Take care of yourselves, and find that little Princess soon! Perhaps you will get her today!'

'Goodbye!' cried the children, and waved to the cuckoo as she rose into the air, her slippered feet tucked well under her, and a little bit of the red shawl hanging down from under her wing. They watched her until they could see her no longer.

Then they turned to look at the market-place. Now, the next thing to do was to find out where Sly-One the gnome lived!

CHAPTER SIX

In the Land of Storytellers

Long-eared gnomes were talking all around them. Nobody took the slightest notice of the two children. They went up to a tall gnome with a long beard and spoke to him.

'Good morning! Please could you tell us something?'

'Anything you like!' said the gnome at once, most politely.

'Could you tell us where the gnome Sly-One lives?' asked Peter.

'Certainly,' answered the long-bearded gnome. 'Do you see that big building over there, with the plants in tubs outside? Well, he lives there.'

'Does he?' said Peter doubtfully. 'It looks like a concert hall or something to me. Does he really live there?'

80

'Haven't I said so?' said the gnome, frowning so crossly that Peter started back in alarm.

'All right, all right!' said the boy, waving the gnome away. 'I believe you! Thanks very much!'

He took Mary's hand and they went to the big building. The great doors were open and they went inside. How strange! It certainly was exactly like a concert hall, for there were rows and rows of chairs there. There was a bent gnome sweeping the floor and Peter went up to him.

'Where can I find the gnome Sly-One?' he asked politely.

'Never heard of him,' said the old bent gnome, still sweeping.

'But he lives here!' said Peter.

'No, he doesn't,' said the gnome, sweeping so near Peter's feet that the boy had to jump out of the way. 'Can't you see this is a concert hall? Does it look as if anyone lived here? You're just playing tricks on me. Get away with you!'

He swept his big broom at Peter and over went the little boy, bump! He jumped up, glared angrily at the gnome and ran back to Mary.

'Sly-One doesn't live here,' he told her. 'What a storyteller that long-bearded gnome was in the market-place!'

'Well, come on,' said Mary, anxious to get out

81

of the dark, cold hall. 'We'll ask someone else.'

So they went out into the sunshine again and looked round. Standing in the middle of the road was a gnome policeman, his helmet shining brightly. They went up to him.

'Please could you tell us where the gnome Sly-One lives?' asked Peter.

'Yes,' said the policeman, and he pointed up the street. 'You want to walk up the hill there, and down the other side. Turn to the right at the baker's shop and you'll find it is a house with a bright yellow door.'

'Oh, thank you very much,' said Peter gratefully. He took Mary's hand and off they went up the hill.

'We should have asked that policeman before,' said Peter. 'Policemen always know!'

They reached the top of the hill and went down the other side. They came to a road that led off to the right and turned down it.

'Now we must look for a house with a yellow door,' said Peter.

So they began. The first door was a blue one. The next a green one, and the third one a black one. They went all down one side of the road, and then began on the other side.

And there wasn't a single house with a yellow door! Not one!

'That's strange!' said Peter, puzzled.

'Do you think the gnome's door *used* to be yellow and he's just had it painted another colour?' said Mary.

'Well, we'll ask,' said Peter. So he knocked at the nearest door, and when it was answered by a little gnome servant he asked her politely which door in the road had once been yellow.

'Oh, *all* the doors were yellow yesterday!' said the little servant-gnome with a giggle, and she slammed the door in Peter's face. He stood looking at it, red and angry. Mary pulled his arm.

'The people are all mad!' she said. But Peter suddenly knew better. Why hadn't he thought of it before?

'They're not mad!' he said. 'They're story-tellers! Aren't we in the Land of Storytellers? Well, we can't expect anyone to tell us the truth then!'

'Oh,' said Mary, dismayed. 'Of course! I hadn't thought of that! I suppose everyone will tell us untruths, no matter what we ask them.'

'So goodness knows how we shall find out where Sly-One lives,' groaned Peter. 'Look, Mary – there's a little seat by the roadside. Let's sit down and eat an apple each. If only, *only* we could find someone as nice as that cuckoo! She didn't mind what she did to help us.'

'There aren't many people like that,' said Mary wisely. They sat down on the seat and munched apples. A little boy-gnome ran up and stared at them. He held out his hand for a piece of apple. Peter suddenly thought of an idea. He took another red apple and held it out to the little gnome.

'You can have this if you'll tell me something,

little gnome,' said Peter. 'Where does Sly-One live?'

'He lives in the cave on the hillside yonder,' said the gnome, his eyes gleaming at the sight of the apple. He pointed to where a green hill rose. 'His cave has a round blue door with a big golden knocker on it. That's where old Sly-One lives.'

'Thank you,' said Peter, and he gave the gnome the apple. He ran off munching it.

'Well, it seems as if we've found out at last where Sly-One lives,' said Mary, finishing her apple. 'Come on, Peter, let's go up the hill.'

Off they went. The hill was steep, but a little winding path led upwards, and they followed it. They came to the cave and saw that it had a round blue door fitted into it. There was a bright golden knocker on the front. Peter was just about to knock when Mary saw a notice by the side of the door. She read it.

'The cave of Surly the Bad-Tempered Gnome,' she read. 'Don't ring or knock.'

'Look, Peter,' she said, in surprise. 'Whatever does this notice mean?'

Peter read it too, and then frowned. 'It means that that little boy-gnome has told us a story too,' he said gloomily. 'I shouldn't think Sly-One lives here – unless he lives with Surly! They would make a good pair!'

'Well – shall we knock and see?' said Mary. 'It says, "Don't knock or ring," but surely the knocker must be meant for knocking!'

Peter knocked loudly, for he was now feeling in a very bad temper. The knocker clanged on the door with a most surprising noise. A growl arose from inside, and then the children heard the clatter of quick, angry footsteps. The door was flung open and out came an ugly gnome with the most bad-tempered face that Peter had ever seen. He whirled his arms about and shouted angrily.

'Get away! Be off with you! Run along! Grr-rr-rr-rr!'

'You ought to be a dog!' said Peter, disgusted.

And then, to the children's enormous astonishment, the gnome at once changed into a big dog who ran at them, showing his teeth, and growling fiercely. Peter caught hold of Mary's hand and ran down the hill as fast as he could.

The gnome-dog stopped half-way down, changed into himself again and laughed loudly. Peter and Mary gazed at him and thought he was the most unpleasant person they had ever met.

'Why ever did you say he ought to be a dog?' said Mary. 'It was a dangerous thing to say!'

'Well, how was I to know he'd turn into a dog just because I said that!' said Peter, still feeling cross. 'I expect that horrid little gnome we gave an apple to thought it was a great joke to send us up to Surly's cave. Nasty little creature!'

'What shall we do now?' asked Mary, as they went on down the hill. 'We shall never find out where Sly-One lives at this rate!'

'*I* don't know what to do,' said Peter gloomily. 'We can't get sense or truth out of anyone here. I'm sorry for Fenella if she is living here, poor little girl!'

'Oh, Peter, we *must* think of something,' said

Mary. 'Oh – I know! Couldn't we find someone who doesn't belong to the Land of Storytellers? Then perhaps they would tell us the truth and we could find out what we want to know.'

'That's a good idea, Mary,' said Peter, cheering up at once. 'We ought to be able to see a pixie or a brownie who doesn't belong here but is just visiting. We'd better go back to the market-place. There are more people there.'

So back they went. The market-place was just

as crowded as ever – but, as far as the children could see, there was nobody there but gnomes, and they must belong to the Land of Story-tellers. They looked about everywhere for an odd pixie or a brownie, but not one could they see.

Then suddenly they saw a pedlar carrying a tray open in front of him. It was slung round his neck by a ribbon. The pedlar looked like a pixie and had a jolly, smiling face.

'Look!' said Mary. 'Let's ask *him*! I'm sure he's not a Storyteller.'

So Peter went up to the pedlar, who at once said, in a loud, singsong voice – 'Ribbons, buttons, cottons, silks, hooksaneyes, tapes, scissors, thimbles, ribbons, buttons, cottons, silks, hooksaneyes. . . .'

'You've said it all once!' said Peter. 'Wait, I want to ask you something!'

'Ribbons, buttons, cottons, silks,' began the pedlar again, but Peter wouldn't let him go on.

'STOP!' he shouted. 'Do you know where the gnome Sly-One lives?'

At once the pedlar turned pale and looked all round as if he were afraid of someone hearing what they said.

'Sly-One, did you say?' he said, in a whisper. 'Why do you want to know about *him*?'

'Because he has captured a great friend of ours, and we want to rescue her,' said Peter.

'Oh, I wouldn't go near that gnome, if I were you, really I wouldn't!' said the pedlar earnestly. 'He's very wicked and very powerful. He has turned lots of people into earwigs, slugs and snails.'

'Oh dear!' said Mary, who didn't like the sound of that at all.

'I don't care *what* Sly-One has done,' said Peter stoutly. 'We've just *got* to rescue poor little Fenella. Pedlar, we have asked ever so many people here where the gnome lives and they've all told us wrong. Can you tell us truthfully?'

'Oh, yes,' said the pedlar. 'I don't belong to the Land of Storytellers, you know, so I speak the truth. I wouldn't live here for anything! Why, the people can't even tell you the right time!'

'Well, where does the gnome live?' asked Peter.

'He lives in a very tall castle just on the borders of this country,' said the pedlar. 'It hasn't any doors at all, except one which disappears as soon as Sly-One has gone in or out.'

'Goodness! Then how shall we get in to rescue Fenella?' cried Mary in dismay.

'There are always the windows,' said the pedlar.

'Will you tell us how to get to the castle?' asked Peter.

'I'll come with you, if you like, and show you the way,' said the pedlar obligingly. The children were delighted to hear this. The pedlar made his way down the street with Peter and Mary behind him. As he went, he cried his wares.

'Ribbons, buttons, cottons, silks, hooksan-eyes, tapes, scissors, thimbles. . . .'

The children followed him through the town and out into the countryside beyond. When he had passed all the people he stopped calling out and beamed round at the children.

'My name's Pop-Off the Pedlar,' he said.

'What a strange name!' said Mary. 'Why are you called that?'

'Oh, well, I'm always popping off to different places, you know,' said the pedlar. 'What are *your* names?'

'I'm Peter, and my sister is Mary,' said Peter. 'Is that castle very far, Pop-Off? I'm getting rather hungry.'

The pedlar rummaged about under his silks and cottons and found a paper bag. He handed it to the children.

'There's enough lunch for us all there,' he said. Peter undid the bag. There were tomato sandwiches, slices of currant cake, and some sweets. It was a very nice lunch. They all munched joyfully as they walked along the dusty road. The hedges were white with may, and the cuckoos called loudly all around them. They reminded the children of the cuckoo-in-the-clock, and they did wish she could be with them.

After some time they passed round the foot of a high hill, and there, rising steeply on the further side, was a strange sort of castle. It was more like one great tower than a castle. It rose high up, almost into the clouds. As the children drew near they could see that there was no door at all and that the windows were set so high up it would be impossible to climb up to them.

'Is *that* where Sly-One lives?' asked Peter in dismay.

'It is,' said Pop-Off. 'If the Princess is there she will probably be in the very topmost room of the tower. That's where Sly-One keeps his prisoners.'

'Look!' said Peter suddenly, pointing up to the top of the tower. 'Do you see that handkerchief waving from the window up there, Mary? Surely that must belong to Fenella. Perhaps she has seen us coming!'

'Ribbons and cottons!' said Pop-Off, in excitement, 'that must be the little lady, sure enough! But how in the world are you going to get to her?'

The children walked all round the strange tower-like castle. It was impossible to find a door – and just as impossible to reach a window. If they couldn't get inside, how could they get Fenella out?

They sat down under a bush, so that if the gnome should come along, he would not see them. Then they all frowned and thought hard.

'If only we could borrow a ladder!' said Peter.

'Impossible!' said Pop-Off, at once. He was frowning so hard that the children couldn't see his eyes. Suddenly he leapt to his feet and did an excited sort of jig, crying, 'Ribbons and buttons! Buttons and ribbons! Of course, of course!'

'Pop-Off, whatever is the matter?' said Peter, in surprise. 'Do be quiet. The gnome might hear you!'

Pop-Off sat down in a hurry.

'Well, I've thought of a most marvellous plan,' he said. 'Really wonderful! I've a little friend, a brown sparrow that I once saved from a cat. It always comes to me when I whistle for it. It will help us to save Fenella!'

'Yes, but Pop-Off, how?' said Peter doubtfully.

'Look here!' said the excited pedlar, showing them the rolls of ribbons and tapes in his basket, 'I've got something here much better than a ladder! I've got strong ribbons and tapes that will make a fine rope, long enough and strong enough to rescue anyone!'

'But how will you get it up to that top window?' asked Peter.

'That's where my friend the sparrow comes in!' said Pop-Off gleefully. 'I'll give him a piece of ribbon to take in his beak, and it will be tied to a rope made of tape and ribbon below. He will fly up to the window with it and give it to the Princess. She will draw up the rope, tie it to her bed, or something, and let herself safely down! What do you think of that for a plan!'

'Splendid!' cried the children, delighted. Mary hugged Pop-Off joyfully. Really, what good friends they had found in their adventures!

'First we'll make the rope of ribbons and tapes,' said the pedlar. He quickly unrolled the ribbons and shook out the tapes. The children watched him beginning to plait a strong rope. He did it so quickly that they could hardly see what he was doing – but soon a plaited ribbon-rope began to coil round him as he worked. The children tried to help, but they could not work half so quickly as the excited pedlar, so they soon gave it up, and watched his clever hands weaving in and out.

'You've made miles, I should think!' said the children, at last.

'Well, we want a long rope to reach right up to that high window,' said the pedlar. He looked at the ribbon-rope round him. 'Still I think that's about enough. Now I'll whistle for my little friend!'

He put two fingers into his mouth and gave a long and trilling whistle, repeated three times. The children waited. For three minutes nothing happened – and then they saw a small speck hurtling through the air towards them. It was the little brown sparrow. It chirruped joyfully when it saw Pop-Off, flew on to his shoulder and lovingly pecked at his ear.

'Listen, Bright-eyes,' said Pop-Off to the waiting sparrow. 'I want your help. Do you see that window high up there, with the handkerchief waving from it? Well, I want you to take this little blue ribbon in your beak and fly up there with it. Give it to the person in the room, and she will know what to do with it.'

'Chirrup, chirrup!' said the sparrow, and at once took the end of the ribbon in its beak. It flew away and the children saw it mounting higher and higher towards the little window at the top of the castle, the blue ribbon fluttering out behind it. It flew right in at the window, and then flew out again, without the ribbon.

Someone inside began to haul up the ribbon swiftly, and the ribbon-rope, which was tied on a long way below the ribbon rose higher and higher up the tower walls. The children watched in excitement. Soon Fenella would appear and climb down to them! Dear little Fenella! It would be so lovely to see her again!

CHAPTER SEVEN

Sly-One the Gnome Again!

But Fenella didn't come. Nobody peeped out of the window. The ribbon-rope hung there, moving slightly in the wind. The children wondered what could be happening. Surely Fenella would know what to do?

'Oh, Peter, suppose she is tied up and can't get to the window!' said Mary suddenly. 'Or she may be ill in bed?'

'I didn't think of that,' said Peter, looking upset. 'Well, there's only one thing to do! I shall climb up the rope myself and see what has happened. I can manage to untie Fenella if she is bound, and then together we'll climb down again.'

The brave boy ran to the rope-end and soon began to swarm up. The castle wall was very rough indeed, and he found that he could climb up the wall with his feet and haul on the rope with his hands. It wasn't very difficult. Mary and Pop-Off watched him going higher and higher. At last he reached the topmost window and went in.

He looked round. There was no one there at all! The room was completely empty except for a strong wooden post to which the ribbon-rope was tied. Where was Fenella? Someone must have tied the rope there!

Just then Peter heard a chuckling laugh. He turned and saw, not Fenella, but Sly-One the gnome, coming in at the door! What a fright he got!

'So you thought you'd come and rescue the Princess, did you?' said the gnome. 'Well, she isn't here. I've put her somewhere else! Ho, ho, ho! And now I've got *you* as well!'

Peter ran to the window, meaning to climb down the rope, but the gnome stopped him.

'No, no!' he said. 'Let the others come too! I've been watching you all for some time. Quite a clever idea, this rope brought up by a sparrow. Oh, yes, quite clever! But not clever enough!'

The gnome went to the window and shouted loudly, 'Help! Help!'

Mary and Pop-Off heard, as he meant them to do. They thought it was Peter calling them. Without a moment's pause the two ran to the rope-end. They swarmed up the rope just as Peter had done, and, panting and puffing, reached the topmost window one below the other. The gnome reached out and hauled them in, then he stood and laughed until the tears ran down his wrinkled cheeks!

'You have walked so nicely into my trap!' he said, at last, grinning at the sulky children and the angry pedlar. 'Did you think you could rescue Fenella so easily? No, no, you are no match for a gnome like me!'

'Where is Fenella?' asked Peter fiercely.

'Well, seeing you are all going to stay here as
my prisoners for some years to come, I don't see
that it matters my telling you what you want to
know!' said the gnome. 'She is hidden away in
a deep cave under the Shining Hill, and the
Goblin Dog is guarding her. Ha! ha! There's a
fine piece of news for you! Think that over for
a few hours!'

The horrid gnome walked out of the door and
slammed it. They heard him slipping great bolts
outside and turning a key in the big lock. They
were prisoners! He had snipped the ribbon-
rope, so that they could not escape out of the
window – what in the world were they to do?

'This is dreadful,' said Peter, sitting down on
the floor and putting his head in his hands. 'Just
when we thought we were so near to Fenella!
Now she is goodness knows where, and we are
prisoners too!'

'I know where Shining Hill is,' said the pedlar
gloomily, 'and I've heard of the Goblin Dog.
We could never, never rescue Fenella from
him. He can smell people from five miles away
and he never sleeps. And, ribbons and buttons,
how we are to get away from here I *don't* know!'

All that day the children and the pedlar
stayed in the topmost room of the high castle.

When evening came the gnome opened a sort

of hatch in the great door and pushed through a tray on which were pieces of bread and a jug of water.

The three of them ate their miserable meal in silence. Then they once again wondered how they might escape. Pop-Off leaned out of the window and wondered if he could climb down the castle wall. But it was too dangerous to try.

'We can't get through that great door, and we can't get out of the window,' he groaned. 'It's impossible, quite impossible to escape. We must just make up our minds to stay here.'

The children agreed with him. It *was* impossible to escape. There were only two ways out of the room and neither way could they take. They lay down on the mattress all curled up together for warmth, and soon, tired out with their adventures, they fell asleep.

In the morning they awoke, feeling more hopeful – but as soon as they had once more looked out of the window and felt the strength of the great door they sighed again and knew that escape was out of the question. The gnome opened the hatch and pushed through a jug of milk and some bread and jam, but he said nothing at all. He seemed to be in a hurry.

The children and Pop-Off ate their breakfast

and looked as miserable as could be. If only they had something to *do!*

'If only we had some game to play!' said Mary. 'Haven't you any game of cards, or snakes and ladders in your tray, Pop-Off?

'No,' said Pop-Off. 'I only sell ribbons and buttons and things. Haven't you any marbles, Peter? Surely you may have some in your pocket?'

'I don't think so,' said Peter, feeling in the pockets of his shorts. He turned out everything he had there – a dirty handkerchief, a long piece of string, a squashed toffee, a pencil, a notebook – and a little round pillbox.

'What's in that box?' said Pop-Off.

'I've forgotten,' said Peter. He opened the box and stared at the fine purple powder inside, puzzled. Where could it have come from? He had quite forgotten. But Mary knew! She gave a loud scream of joy, and made Peter jump so much that he nearly spilt the powder.

'Peter! Peter! Don't you remember? It's the box of powder that our mother gave us! She said it might come in useful some day. Oh, Peter, perhaps it will save us!'

Peter's face brightened up. Of course! But how could the powder help them? He didn't know what it could do or was meant to do.

'Let me look at it,' said Pop-Off suddenly. He looked at the powder carefully and then smelt it. Then he tasted a tiny bit and quickly spat it out.

'I do believe – I – do believe –' he began in great excitement, 'it's Disappearing Powder!'

'Whatever do you mean?' asked the children, astonished.

'Wait a moment,' said the pedlar. He took up a little of the powder and spread it on to a silver thimble that he took from his tray. As the children watched they saw, to their amazement, that the thimble seemed to be crumbling away into thin fine powder, so fine that when Pop-Off blew it, it flew into smoke and disappeared before their eyes!

'There you are, I was right!' said Pop-Off, in the greatest delight. 'It *is* Disappearing Powder. It makes things disappear!'

'Well, shall we spread it over ourselves and make ourselves disappear, then?' said Mary.

'Of course not!' said Pop-Off scornfully. 'Whatever would be the use of that? We'd vanish completely and never come back!'

'Well – how can we use the powder to help us, then?' asked Peter.

'We'll rub it on the great door!' said Pop-Off, grinning joyfully. 'It will make it disappear – or any rate part of it will vanish, a big enough piece to make a hole for us to squeeze through. We'll be able to escape after all!'

The children stared at him, their eyes wide with amazement. Of course! How clever of Pop-Off to think of such a thing! What a good thing he happened to be there with them, for they themselves would never have thought that the powder could do a strange thing like that!

'We'll wait until the gnome has given us our midday meal,' said Pop-Off, planning hard. 'Then, when we think everything is safe we'll make a hole in the door with the purple powder, creep through it, run down the stairs and find a way of getting out of the Tower.'

'But there aren't any doors to it!' said Peter.

'Oh, never mind!' said Pop-Off. '*We'll* find a way, once we're out of this horrid little room!'

Peter put the box safely away in his pocket. Then they sat and waited patiently until Sly-One came with their dinner. He came at last, thrust a tray through the hatchway in the door, chuckled hoarsely to see their three pale faces, and disappeared.

On the tray were meat sandwiches, three slices of bread, and a big jug of water. The children and Pop-Off ate hungrily, and then looked excitedly at one another. Was it safe to try the powder?

'I should think we might try now,' said Pop-Off at last. He took the box from Peter, emptied a little of the powder into his hand and began to rub it on to a small piece of the door, rather low down. The children watched, excited. After a while that part of the door seemed to crumble away, and the three could quite well see through the hole it made! The pedlar blew hard and the crumbling piece flew into smoke.

Again Pop-Off rubbed more powder on to the next piece of the door and again the same thing happened. It crumbled away and a bigger hole still came!

'I do hope we have enough powder to make a hole big enough for us to squeeze through!' said Peter.

'Oh, plenty, I should think!' said Pop-Off, blowing away more of the crumbling wood into smoke. He went on with his work, and by the time he had used all the powder in the little round box there was a fine big hole in the door! Mary knew that she and Peter could easily squeeze through it, and she hoped that Pop-Off could too. He was bigger than they were.

'Now!' said Pop-Off at last. 'Let's get through! But mind! Not a scrap of noise! I'll get through first, and you two follow.'

He began to crawl through the hole. His tray stuck sideways and he took it off and gave it to Peter to hold. Then he managed to get right through easily. Peter tipped the tray up and just got it through the door, too. Pop-Off slipped it over his neck again.

Peter went next and then Mary. They stood outside the great door and looked round them in silence. They were on a small landing, set with doors like their own. Before them stretched a long, steep flight of stairs, thickly carpeted.

'Down we go!' whispered Pop-Off, and set off

down the stairs. The others followed. Down they went and down and down. Would the stairs never come to an end?

They passed many, many doors, all of which were shut. Strange noises came from behind some of them – whirrings and whinings, growlings and snortings. The children wondered what was in the rooms and hoped that none of the doors would open as they passed!

One door did swing open! Out of the room peeped a large cat with green whiskers. Its eyes opened wide as it saw the three creeping down the stairs. It was just going to mew loudly, when Pop-Off stepped up to it and raised his fist so fiercely that the cat, with a frightened squeak, shut the door quickly. Pop-Off saw a key in the lock and quick as thought he turned it and grinned at the others.

'He won't be able to give the alarm!' he whispered. 'He's safe there for a little while!'

On and on went the pedlar and the children, creeping silently down the endless stairs. And at last they came to a great hall, hung with curtains of all colours. Pop-Off held out his hand to stop the others and carefully peeped round the bend of the stairs to see if anyone was there.

Sly-One was sitting at the table, eating a good dinner!

Pop-Off stared in dismay. Now what were they to do? He took a look at the thick curtains that hung all round the hall. Perhaps they could hide behind those. He made the children understand, by nods and pointings, what his idea was.

Sly-One made a great deal of noise as he ate. He had very bad manners. Pop-Off thought this was a good thing as perhaps the noise he made would prevent him from hearing the children creeping behind the curtains. He slipped behind them first and then Mary followed him silently. Just as Peter was going too a reel of cotton fell from the pedlar's tray and dropped on the floor!

The gnome stopped eating and cocked his head on one side.

'What's that?' he said aloud. 'Did I drop something?' He looked on the floor, but could see nothing.

'Must have been a mouse!' he said, and went on with his dinner. Peter slipped behind the curtains too, and all three trembled and shook because of their narrow escape.

The gnome finished his dinner. He yawned widely, with his arms above his head.

'Now for a good long nap!' he said. He went to a couch and lay down, first taking off his pointed slippers. He covered himself with a rug and shut his eyes. In half a minute the children heard long snores, almost as loud as the giants had made two nights before!

'Now's our chance!' whispered Pop-Off, peeping out. 'We must see if there's a way to get out.'

'This hall is hung all the way round with curtains,' said Mary, looking about her. 'There doesn't seem to be any window at all, and certainly no doors.'

'Unless they are somewhere in the wall behind the curtains,' said Pop-Off. 'There might be secret, hidden doors there. After all, the gnome must get in and out of the castle *some*how!'

So, on tiptoe, the children felt all the way round the walls behind the great coloured curtains. They came right back to the place where they had started – but not a door was to be seen! It was most disappointing.

'We haven't any of that Disappearing Powder left, have we?' said Mary in a whisper. 'We could make a hole through the walls if we had.'

'There's not even a grain!' said Pop-Off. 'I used it all up, every bit.'

They stood behind the curtains and looked in dismay at one another. Whatever were they to do?

Then Mary's sharp eyes caught sight of something in the middle of the floor of the hall. It was a large trapdoor!

'Look!' she whispered in excitement. 'Isn't that a trapdoor? Couldn't we get through it and escape that way before the gnome wakes up?'

The others stared at the trapdoor. Yes – it certainly did look like a way of escape! How marvellous!

The gnome still snored steadily. Pop-Off thought that there would never be a better time to escape than now. 'We'll risk it!' he whispered. 'Now, not the slightest sound, remember!'

They left the shelter of the thick curtains and

tiptoed across to the trapdoor. There was a big ring to pull it up, and Pop-Off took hold of it. He tugged – and the trapdoor came up easily and lightly. It was plain that it was used very often!

Below there was a flight of steps, stretching down into the darkness. Pop-Off wondered how they would see. He saw a candle and a box of matches lying on the gnome's table and tiptoed up to get them. At least they would have a light!

Peter went through the trapdoor first and then Mary followed. Pop-Off was just climbing through too when the ribbon that tied his tray round his neck caught on a nail and the tray tipped up. A dozen reels and skeins fell through the trapdoor and bounced down the steps!

The gnome woke up at once and looked round. Pop-Off hurriedly untwisted the ribbon from the nail, took a frightened look at the astonished gnome and then lowered himself at top speed through the trapdoor. The gnome sprang up with a roar of rage and rushed over to him.

Pop-Off pulled the trapdoor to with a clang. He hung on to it underneath, feeling the gnome pulling for all he was worth. Then Peter lighted the candle and Pop-Off saw, to his great delight, that there were two strong bolts on the underneath of the trapdoor. He shot them at once and let go his hold on the bottom part of the door. The gnome could not open it now!

'Quick! We'd better go whilst we've got the chance!' he said to the children. 'The gnome may find some way of getting through. He's clever enough, goodness knows!'

Sly-One was beside himself with rage. The children could hear him dancing about on the trapdoor, shouting and yelling in his harsh voice.

'He's saying something about the Goblin Dog,' said Peter. 'It sounds as if he's saying that it will eat us.'

'Rubbish!' said Pop-Off. 'The Dog is in the Shining Hill, far away.'

The little candle gave them enough light to see by as they made their way down the steps and through a dark and winding passage. Sometimes the passage opened out into caves and then closed again into a narrow way between dark rocks. It was cold and damp – but at any rate they had escaped! That was something to be thankful for!

'This must lead somewhere,' said Pop-Off hopefully. 'Perhaps we shall come to a signpost or something soon, which will tell us where we are going.'

And after a while they did. The signpost stood in a cave and had two arms. One pointed back to where they had come from and said 'To Sly-One's Castle.'

The other one pointed forward. When the children read it, what a shock they got!

This is what it said – "To the Cave of the Goblin Dog!'

'Buttons and ribbons!' said Pop-Off, in the greatest dismay. 'Who would have thought of that! That's what the gnome was shouting about, I suppose – saying we would be eaten by the Goblin Dog!'

'There is no way but these two ways,' said Peter. 'Either we go back to Sly-One – or we go forward to the Goblin Dog. Whatever shall we do?'

'Well, we were going to the Shining Hill to find the Dog's Cave anyhow,' said Mary, 'so we might as well go on. Fenella's there.'

'That's true,' said Peter. 'But it doesn't sound very nice, somehow.'

'Come on!' said Pop-Off suddenly. 'We're out of the frying pan and into the fire, it seems to me – but we may as well make the best of it and be brave!'

So on into the darkness they went, lighted by the yellow flame of their little candle.

CHAPTER EIGHT

In the Shining Hill with the Goblin Dog

They went through caves and passages again, and were glad of their candle, for there was no light anywhere – but at last, when their candle was almost burnt right down and they were all feeling tired, they came to a curious cave.

The walls shone brightly and lighted up the way so that they could see without their candle. Glittering stones sparkled in the walls of the caves, and Peter and Mary gazed at them in wonder. Surely they must be very precious stones!

They went on through more and more caves, all lighted by the same shining in the walls, the shining of hundreds of brilliant stones. Peter stopped and tried to get some of the stones out of the walls.

'What do you want those for?' asked the pedlar impatiently.

'Well, I thought that they would make a lovely present for the Lady Rozabel, and if I take some for my father, he could sell them and become a rich man,' said Peter, busily prising the stones away from the walls. He put a few dozens into his pocket, pleased with his find. If ever they got home safely how rich he would be!

'This is a wonderful place,' said Mary, as they walked on, lighted by the glittering stones all round them.

'It must be the inside of the Shining Hill,' said Pop-Off. 'It shines like this on the outside, too, but no one dares to go near it, because the Goblin Dog lives there. He is such a fierce creature.'

'Poor Fenella! I hope she isn't too unhappy,' said Peter.

They went on and on – and then suddenly they stopped. A dreadful noise came to their ears! It was like the barking and yelping of a hundred dogs!

'That's the Goblin Dog,' said Pop-Off. 'He's smelt us already. My goodness, we'd better be careful!'

'How can we be careful?' said Mary. 'We've *got* to go on. We can't go back!'

'That's true,' said Pop-Off mournfully. He

went on again, on tiptoe, peeping round corners carefully, as if expecting the Dog to come round any moment. It was very frightening! At last they rounded a shining corner and came out into a huge cave, lighted from end to end by the brightly glittering stones – and there, in the middle of it, stood a great dog, his eyes glittering like the stones, his big ears pricked up, his long and snake-like tail lashing to and fro like a cat's.

He barked – and how he barked! It was really deafening. He showed his teeth and the children gazed in horror. How could they hope to get Fenella away from such a fierce creature!

'Where is Fenella?' shouted Peter bravely.

'What's that to do with you?' growled the Goblin Dog, lashing his tail all the more fiercely.

Peter looked all round. There was no sign of Fenella. Where could she be?

'We want the Princess Fenella!' he shouted to the dog. 'Tell us where she is at once!'

'I shan't and I won't!' barked the Dog, and he showed his teeth again.

'Better not get him into a temper,' whispered Pop-Off, who was feeling very nervous.

'Well, I *must* find out what has become of the Princess!' said Peter. 'You look after Mary,

Pop-Off. I'm going to show that Dog that I mean what I say!'

Without showing the least signs of fear Peter stalked right up to the Dog. He was almost knocked down by the lashing tail, but he folded his arms, looked the Goblin Dog straight in the eye and yelled at him:

'WHERE IS FENELLA?'

'Where *you* can't find her, or Sly-One either!' said the Dog angrily.

'But aren't you guarding her for Sly-One?' cried Peter in surprise.

'Never you mind what I'm doing!' said the Dog. 'If you don't turn round, all of you, and go back the way you came, I'll bite you!'

He certainly looked as if he would. But Peter did not stir. That made the Dog angry and he suddenly leapt at the small boy, who was knocked over before he could get out of the way. He shouted, and Pop-Off ran to the rescue. But the Dog stood over him, growling.

Then, to everyone's enormous surprise, a sweet, soft voice cried, 'Goblin Dog! What is all the noise about?'

'That's Fenella's voice!' cried Peter.

'And that's Peter's voice!' cried Fenella, and scrambling through a hole in the cave wall came the little Princess herself. She flung herself on

Mary and Peter and cried tears of joy. The Goblin Dog stood watching in amazement.

'Oh, Goblin Dog!' said Fenella reproachfully, 'I do hope you didn't frighten my friends. They have come to rescue me, I'm sure.'

'I thought they were enemies,' mumbled the Dog, drooping his tail and ears, and looking thoroughly ashamed of himself. 'I thought I was protecting you. How did I know but what they might be friends of Sly-One? They didn't say who they were.'

Peter stared in amazement. Wasn't the Goblin Dog keeping Fenella a prisoner for Sly-One, then?

'I don't understand,' said the boy. 'Fenella, isn't the Dog keeping you prisoner?'

'He was at first,' said Fenella, 'but I soon found out that he was a kind-hearted creature, and we became friends. Then he said he would protect me if Sly-One came to fetch me. Isn't that right, Dog dear?'

The great creature put out his tongue and licked the little Princess gently.

'I love Fenella,' he said, in a yelping voice. 'She is the only person who has ever been kind to me, or hasn't thought me ugly. Sly-One has always kept me here in these caves, for he said I was too ugly to be seen outside. So I grew fierce and lonely and hated everyone.'

'You're *not* ugly!' said Fenella, stroking his rough coat. 'You're the dearest, kindest, beautifullest dog that ever was, and I'd like to take you home with me and let you live in a lovely kennel in the palace yard!'

The Goblin Dog lay down on his back and rolled over in delight. Pop-Off and the children were too astonished to say a word. No wonder the Dog had been so fierce when he thought they had come to take Fenella back to Sly-One!

Peter patted him. 'If you're Fenella's friend, you're ours too,' he said. 'We all like dogs, especially a good, kind dog like you. Can you

tell me how to get out of here without going back through the gnome's castle?'

'Oh, do tell me all your adventures!' said Fenella, pulling at Peter's arm, before the Dog could say a word. 'Do tell me how you got here! Oh, it's too wonderful to see you all again. I have been so lonely and unhappy, first in that horrid gnome's castle, and then down here in these caves. I really don't know what I would have done without my kind Goblin Dog!'

The Dog licked Fenella again and then gambolled happily round the cave. It was full of delight to have so many friends round it.

122

'Well, is there time to stop and tell our adventures?' said Peter doubtfully. 'Oughtn't we to try and escape whilst we can?'

'Oh, we've got the Goblin Dog to protect us now,' said Fenella. 'Come and see the little cave I've got all to myself here. I was just going to have my tea. You can all have some with me. That would be lovely!'

She scrambled through the hole in the cave wall once more and everyone followed her, the Goblin Dog nearly getting stuck in it, for he was so big. On the other side was a cosy cave, its walls hung with red curtains. A small bed stood on one side, and a table and some stools were here and there. A little stove was in one corner and a kettle was boiling there.

It was strange to have tea in a small cave in the heart of the Shining Mountain. Fenella poured out the tea, and put plenty of sugar into everybody's cup. There was bread and butter and jam and a big fruit cake.

Whilst they were eating, Peter, Mary and Pop-Off told Fenella and the Dog all the adventures they had had. How the princess squealed when she heard how they had escaped from the giants! How she opened her eyes when she listened to the tale of Peter climbing up the tower wall, helped by the ribbon-rope – only to find

123

the gnome in the room where he had hoped to find the little Princess herself!

'I did tie my handkerchief to the window,' said Fenella. 'I hoped, if anyone came to rescue me, they would see it flying there and know that it was a signal. I suppose the gnome heard that you were on the way, and hid me here, then waited for you to come, the horrid thing!'

'We didn't guess that you would make friends with the Goblin Dog,' said Peter. 'We were dreadfully worried about you.'

'How could I help making friends with him!' said Fenella, patting the Dog on the head and giving him a very large slice of fruit cake which he swallowed at one gulp. 'He's a pet!'

'I like him too,' said Mary, and the Goblin Dog hung out his tongue at her and panted with delight. He had very large, soft brown eyes, and, though he certainly was a strange and ugly dog, there *was* something very likeable about him. Pop-Off wasn't quite sure of him, but Peter felt certain he was a good-hearted animal, who had only turned fierce and disagreeable because people had been unkind to him.

They were just finishing tea very happily together when the Goblin Dog suddenly leapt to his feet, barked madly and lashed his tail about violently. It hit the teapot and knocked it over so that it smashed to bits.

'Goblin Dog, what's the matter?' cried Fenella, in astonishment. 'Look what you've done! You've broken the teapot! Oh, what a mess!'

The Goblin Dog took no notice of Fenella at all. He just went on barking as if he had gone quite mad. His tail swished about more quickly than ever and the children got hurriedly out of its way, for it was strong enough to knock them over.

The Dog growled and showed his teeth, his eyes gleaming, looking towards the hole through which the children had scrambled. Everyone began to feel frightened. Whatever had happened to the Dog?

'Is it someone coming?' asked Pop-Off suddenly.

'It's Sly-One. I can smell him,' said the Dog, with a low, fierce growl. Everyone was startled. Sly-One! He must have found some way of opening the trapdoor and come down after all.

'What shall we do?' said Peter. 'Dog, is there any way of getting out of this mountain except through the caves that lead to Sly-One's tower?'

'There's one other way,' said the Dog. 'There is a deep-sunk well not far from this cave. It goes right down from the house on the top of the mountain, to far below where we are standing now, for water. There is a hole that enters the well, a good way above the water. If we can get there, and one of us could get to the top, he could let down the bucket and take us all up to the top, one by one.'

'Let's try that way, then,' said Pop-Off eagerly. He didn't at all want to face the gnome again.

'Come along then, quickly,' said the Dog. 'Sly-One is a good way away yet.'

He led the way. Through winding passages, as dark as night except for the glittering stones here and there in the rock, went all the five, hurrying as much as they could. The Dog went first, and Peter went last, looking back every now and again to make sure the gnome was not near.

'Here we are!' said the Dog at last. They crowded round a small hole in the cave wall and peered through it. Far down below they saw the gleam of inky-black water. Above them rose the rounded walls of the old well. By leaning right through the hole and looking upwards Pop-Off could see a little spot of daylight — the top of the well. That made him feel most excited. If only they could get into the open air again!

'How are we going to get up?' he said. 'There is no way, except by climbing.'

'Couldn't you whistle for your little sparrow friend again, and let him fly up with another ribbon-rope?' cried Peter.

Pop-Off shook his head very dolefully. 'No, that's no good,' he said. 'I used all my good ribbon for the other rope. I haven't nearly enough left now.'

Fenella looked at the Goblin Dog's feet. She knew that he had long, sharp claws, much more like a cat's than a dog's. She put her arm round his neck and spoke coaxingly to him.

'Goblin Dog, you are very clever, and you have claws like a cat. Couldn't you climb up the well yourself? You are such a wonderful dog that I am sure you could do anything!'

The Goblin Dog swelled with pride to hear Fenella speak to him like that. He shot out all his long, curved claws and put up his ears.

'I'll try, Princess dear,' he said, and licked her little pink nose. 'I'd do anything in the world for you! I'll try to get right up to the top, and then I'll let down the bucket for you and draw you up again.'

He scrambled through the hole and began to climb up the rough bricked sides of the well. The bricks were very rough and uneven and he

found foothold easily enough – but the bricks were old and, as his weight rested on them, some of them crumbled away and fell with a deep splash into the water far below.

The four left behind watched with beating hearts. Suppose the Dog fell? He would tumble far down to the water, and how would he get out? More bricks fell and every time the bits came hurtling down everyone thought the Dog was falling too.

But fortunately he had twenty strong claws to climb with, and as he was quite fearless, he didn't at all bother about what would happen if he fell. He just went on climbing. Soon he grew hot and tired, and Peter and the others could hear him panting and puffing as he struggled upwards towards the spot of light.

'I hope he gets to the top before the gnome comes,' said Peter nervously. 'It wouldn't be very nice to have the gnome capturing us again, without the Dog to protect us!'

Soon they couldn't hear anything of the Dog, for he was so far up the well. Pop-Off leaned out into the well shaft and said that he couldn't see the spot of light at the top. The Dog must be there!

Presently there came a clinking-clanking sound and to everyone's delight a big bucket came down the well! Pop-Off caught it as it swung down on its rope, and stopped it. The rope was tightened from above, where the Dog was holding it. He had climbed up quite safely and had let down the bucket!

'Good old Dog!' said Fenella. 'I knew he'd do it! I shall certainly have him for a pet when I get home again.'

'Come on, now,' said Pop-Off, impatient to get out of the dark heart of the mountain. 'Fenella and Mary first. There's room for you both!'

The two girls climbed in and pulled on the rope. Immediately the bucket began to rise up the well. Up and up it went, as the Dog wound the handle of the well – up and up, up and up. And at last, there it was at the top, and there was the Goblin Dog beaming all over his ugly face at them.

'You're a dear!' said Fenella. 'Now let the bucket down again for the others.'

Down it went. Pop-Off and Peter were impatiently awaiting it. Would it never come?

Pop-Off heard a sound in the caves behind them. He listened. It was the noise of running feet and panting breath. It could only be the gnome, looking for them all! His heart beat fast. He saw that Peter had heard too. They kept as quiet as mice. Oh, if only the bucket would come in time!

Nearer and nearer the sounds came. Pop-Off looked up the well. The bucket was coming down, thank goodness, but how slow it seemed. It arrived at last and Pop-Off pushed Peter into it. He was just climbing in himself when the gnome arrived, panting and breathless, yelling for the Goblin Dog!

'Goblin Dog! Where are you? What have you done with Fenella? Goblin Dog, come HERE!'

He caught sight of the hole in the cave, and saw Pop-Off's scared face turned to him as he settled himself in the bucket.

'Pull, Dog, pull!' yelled Pop-Off, hoping to goodness that the Dog would hear him. The bucket began to go up, swinging from side to side on the end of the rope. Sly-One poked his head through the hole and stared in amazement up the well. He had no idea of such a way of escape. He could hardly believe his eyes.

Then he began to shake his fist and shout angry things. Pop-Off, feeling safe, shouted back. This made the gnome so angry that he leaned too far through the hole and fell down into the well! Down, down, down, he went, and then splash, he was in the icy water! Pop-Off laughed till he cried, but Peter was scared.

'Can he get out?' he asked.

'Oh, yes!' said Pop-Off, wiping his tears away. 'He can use some of the precious magic he knows, and he'll do it quickly too, for he'll want to be after us again, I've no doubt! He will hope to catch us all before we get Fenella safely home! Don't worry your head about *him*, Peter!'

CHAPTER NINE

An Exciting Escape

At the top of the well all the five looked at one another thankfully.

'Well, we've escaped,' said Pop-Off, wiping his forehead with a big red handkerchief.

'Thanks to the good old Goblin Dog!' said Fenella, giving him a hug, at which he was very pleased.

'Where exactly are we now?' asked Mary, looking round her. 'Look, there's a cottage over there. Let's go and ask where we are.'

They went up to the little cottage and knocked at the door. It opened – and oh dear, who should be there but the Green Wizard, Sly-One's best friend! The Goblin Dog knew him at once, and whispered to the others.

'Ah!' said the Green Wizard, smiling round. 'Pray come in!'

But nobody wanted to! They didn't trust the

133

Green Wizard – and he might ask them some very awkward questions! They were sure he had recognized Fenella.

'You must have a cup of tea with me,' said the Wizard. 'I shall be very much offended if you don't. And I'm not a very nice person then, you know. Come in, do – I'll put the kettle on.'

There didn't seem anything else to do. They went into the cottage in silence. The wizard took up a kettle, and then looked annoyed.

'No water!' he said. 'Pardon me a minute – I'll get some from the well! It won't take a minute to let down the bucket.'

He ran out of the cottage with the kettle and went over to the well.

'My goodness! Sly-One is still at the bottom!' said Pop-Off. 'He'll come up in the bucket!'

They all felt very worried. They stood and looked at the wizard winding the chain of the bucket. It must have reached the bottom of the well by now. Then he began to draw it up again – and dear me – it seemed as if it was very heavy indeed!

'Suppose Sly-One's in the bucket – what shall we do?' said Peter, in dismay.

'Run, of course!' said Mary.

'But we'll never out-run the gnome!' said Pop-Off.

'*I* know,' said Fenella. 'The Goblin Dog is big and strong enough to take us all on his back and run with us, aren't you, Dog?'

'Certainly,' said the Dog, willing to do anything for the little Princess. 'Look – the bucket is coming to the top now.'

They all watched – and, just as they had feared, the gnome Sly-One had climbed into the bucket and had come up with the water! He leapt out in a furious rage and began to talk to the wizard, who listened in the greatest amazement. Then he pointed towards his house and the gnome grinned in delight.

'He's told him we're here!' groaned Pop-Off. 'Come on everybody, we must run!'

They rushed out of the back door. One by one they climbed up on to the broad back of the Goblin Dog, held tight to his hairs, and off they went, at top speed.

The Green Wizard and Sly-One came running out of the back door in a fury, when they found that Fenella and the others had gone. They saw the Dog rushing away with all the rest on his back, and the gnome danced with rage. Then he and the wizard ran indoors.

'They're up to some mischief or other!' said Pop-Off, looking back. 'They'll be after us before long!'

On went the Dog, galloping on his four feet, and everyone clung tightly. He went very fast indeed and Mary thought that surely no one could ever catch them up!

'The gnome and the wizard are after us!' cried Pop-Off suddenly. 'They've got a cat from Giantland, bigger than a donkey, and they're tearing along at a fearful rate!'

It was quite true. The giant cat covered the ground tremendously fast, and Pop-Off began to think it would catch them up.

'Faster, faster!' he cried – and the Goblin

Dog galloped more furiously than ever. The children had hard work to keep on his back, and if Fenella hadn't discovered two hard knobbly things sticking out of the Dog's back, she would certainly have fallen off. She held on to the knobs, wondering whatever they were.

Then a dreadful thing happened! The Dog suddenly tumbled, gave a yelp of pain and began to limp.

'What's the matter?' cried Pop-Off.

'It's a thorn in my foot,' groaned the poor Goblin Dog, limping along on three legs.'

'Stop a minute and I'll get it out for you,' called Pop-Off. The Dog stopped and Pop-Off slipped off his back. The Dog held up his foot and Pop-Off saw a big thorn there. He took a pair of tweezers from his tray and pulled out the thorn. But alas, the Dog's foot was so sore that he could hardly put it to the ground!

Pop-Off gave a despairing look back at the giant cat, who was swiftly coming nearing with the yelling gnome and wizard on its back. Then Fenella called to him.

'Pop-Off! What are these lumps on the Dog's back?'

Pop-Off looked and gave a howl of joy. 'Goblin Dog! You've never grown your wings! All Goblin Dogs can do that! Grow them now,

137

whilst I rub the knobs and say the magic words. Then you can fly!'

'I'd love to,' said the Dog, pleased. 'I've always wanted wings, but Sly-One never would let me grow them.'

Pop-Off began to rub the knobs and chanted a string of strange magic words as he did so. To the children's enormous surprise the knobs grew larger. Then they burst like flower buds and out of them unfolded great yellow wings covered with large blue spots and circles. It was marvellous! The Goblin Dog flapped them proudly.

'Quick, get on again!' he called. We shall be caught unless I get away now!'

They all scrambled on, horrified to see how near the gnome and the wizard were. Then up into the air rose the Goblin Dog, flapping his enormous yellow wings, and going along at a great rate. Pop-Off looked down and saw the gnome and the wizard looking up at them in dismay. Their giant cat could not fly!

But Sly-One was not so easily beaten. He clapped his hands seven times and called out some magic words. And hey presto, his giant cat grew four pairs of wings and rose up into the air! He could fly as well as the Goblin Dog!

'Quick, Goblin Dog, quick!' shouted Pop-

Off, and the Dog panted loudly as he flew. Peter looked down desperately. Oh to see the bright towers and spires of Fairyland!

Then he suddenly gave a loud shout. 'Look! Look! Can you see what I see? There, in the distance? It's Fairyland, it's Fairyland!'

'Home! Home!' shouted Fenella. 'Hurry, dear Goblin Dog, hurry. We'll soon be home.'

But the Goblin Dog was getting tired. He had a heavy load on his back, and his wings flapped more and more slowly. At last, as he was nearing Fairyland, he flew so slowly that Pop-Off was certain the Giant Cat would catch them up. Then a fine and unselfish idea came into his head.

'Goblin Dog, fly down to the ground and let me, Peter and Mary get off,' he said. 'Then you fly on to Fairyland with Fenella – you'll fly much more quickly then.'

At once the dog obeyed. Fenella cried and said no, she wouldn't go without them, but Peter was firm and set her safely on the Dog's back. Then up they went together, the Dog and Fenella, and Pop-Off was glad to see how much faster they flew now that the Dog had a lighter load.

He pulled the others under a bush, for the Giant Cat was passing over. The Cat circled overhead for a few minutes to find out if anything was to be seen – but as the three of them kept perfectly still, it soon flew off again after the dog and Fenella.

'Now we must make our way home again as fast as we can,' said Peter. 'Please come with us, Pop-Off. My mother will be so pleased to know you when she hears what a friend you have been.'

'Well, I'd like to see you safely back home,' said the pedlar. 'So I'll come.'

CHAPTER TEN

Everything Comes Right Again

Now down below in Fairyland there was great excitement, for many people had seen the Goblin Dog in the distance. They ran to tell Lord Rolland, and he at once gave orders that fairy archers were to shoot at the Dog and bring it down.

'Goblin Dogs are wicked creatures, who help bad witches and gnomes to do their evil deeds,' said Lord Rolland. 'We will catch this one and take it prisoner!'

So the archers took up their bows and arrows and shot at the coming Goblin Dog. He was astonished when he heard the whizz of arrows through the air – and poor thing, he did not know what to do! He did not dare to turn and go back, for if he did he would fly straight into the Giant Cat! No, he must fly through the cloud of arrows and see if he could bring the little Princess safely to earth!

So the brave dog flew on, yelping whenever a sharp arrow pierced his big wings. Fenella clasped her arms around him, sobbing, for she knew what was happening and was dreadfully afraid that her dear kind dog would be hurt. Just as the Dog was about to fly over the walls of Fairyland an arrow caught him at the root of his right wing and he fell, unable to fly. He flapped with his left wing and managed to reach the ground safely with Fenella, just outside the gates of Fairyland.

At once the golden gates were flung open and out rushed a crowd of fairies, meaning to drag in the Dog to Lord Rolland – but when they saw Fenella climbing off his back they shouted in wonder and amazement.

'Fenella! The little Princess! Fenella!'

They rushed to her, took her hands and began to pull her into Fairyland. Above them they suddenly heard the rush of wings and looking up, they saw the great Giant Cat with the angry gnome and wizard peering down from its back.

At once the archers set their arrows to their bows and sent a hundred whizzing up into the air! The Giant Cat gave a yell and turned back at once, in spite of the angry shouts of the wizard, who tried to make it fly down and take Fenella from the fairies. No, the Giant Cat had had quite enough. It flew off steadily, giving little squeals.

The archers shot their arrows after it. The wizard suddenly gave a shout and clapped his hand to his leg. Then the gnome gave a yell and clapped his hand to his nose. Both had been struck by arrows!

'Serves them right!' said Fenella, who was watching. 'Nasty, horrid things! They deserve it! That will teach them not to come back again!'

'Oh, Fenella, dear little Fenella, come quickly to the Lady Rozabel, your mother!' cried all the fairies, and they tugged at her hands and arms, and ran through the gates. She pulled back, looking towards the Goblin Dog, who lay panting, his hurt wing stretched out flat beside him.

'I must go back to the Goblin Dog and see if he is hurt,' she said.

'No, no, he is a dreadful, horrid creature!' cried all the little folk at once. 'Leave him! We will see to him. Look! Look! There is your mother!'

At the sight of her mother the Princess forgot all about the Goblin Dog and rushed to the

Lady Rozabel. She hugged her mother and cried happy tears all down her cheeks.

'Come and see your father!' said Lady Rozabel, who was weeping for joy too. 'He does not know you are here! Oh, Fenella, darling Fenella, to think you are really home again at last!'

Fenella cried with happiness to see her own home again. She was so tired that she could

hardly keep her eyes open, but she wanted to tell her mother all her adventures – and especially she wanted the Goblin Dog fetched into Fairyland. But the Lady Rozabel would not let her tell anything that night. 'You are so tired, Fenella darling,' she said. 'Come to bed. Tomorrow you shall say all you want to.'

'But my Goblin Dog,' murmured Fenella, her eyes almost closing.

'We will see to the Goblin Dog,' said Lord Rolland grimly. He had no idea that the Dog had helped Fenella so much. He thought that it had flown with her by command of that gnome who had followed on the Giant Cat. He kissed the little Princess and hurried out to give his orders.

In a trice the little folk surrounded the surprised Goblin Dog, who had been patiently awaiting Fenella to come and fetch him and bathe his wing. They tied him up tightly, and took him to prison, threatening him with all sorts of dreadful punishments. He didn't know *what* to think. He was very unhappy.

The little folk dragged him to a prison cell and locked him up there. He was thirsty and hungry, and his wing hurt him – but no one paid him any more attention. They all thought that he was a wicked Goblin Dog, servant of the gnome who had taken Fenella away. So there he was left, sad and lonely, all night long!

And what about Pop-Off, Peter and Mary? Well, as soon as the Giant Cat had flown off with the gnome and the wizard, they crawled out from under their bush and looked round.

'I know where we are!' cried Peter joyfully. 'We are not very far from our own home. Look, Mary, there's the shepherd's hut that our father often uses in wintertime!'

Gladly they turned towards the little valley in which their own cottage stood. Pop-Off walked with them, wondering if the Goblin Dog had got safely over the borders of Fairyland with Fenella. Suddenly he gave a shout, and pulled the others under a tree.

'The Giant Cat again!' he said. They looked up. Sure enough it was the flying Cat, carrying on its back a squealing gnome and wizard, one rubbing his nose and the other his leg.

'They're going back!' said Pop-Off, pleased. 'That means Fenella is safe. Oh, how lovely! Well, we'll see her tomorrow!'

They walked on, and in two hours' time they came to the valley where their cottage stood. Not far off stood the golden gates of Fairyland. Outside, to the children's enormous surprise, lay the Goblin Dog, his hurt wing outspread beside him! There was no sign of Fenella at all.

'What's happened?' cried Peter, staring. 'Why hasn't the Goblin Dog gone through the gates with Fenella? Oh look – here comes lots of the little folk! Perhaps they are going to cheer the Goblin Dog, and take him into Fairyland.'

But to the children's enormous surprise they saw the Goblin Dog being roughly handled by the little folk, and dragged through the gates, a prisoner!

'I won't have that!' shouted Peter, in a rage, and he rushed down the hill towards the gates, shouting 'Stop! Stop!'

But the fairies did not hear him. They dragged the Dog away and the gates shut. Peter and Mary ran up to them and battered on them until the gatekeeper looked out in surprise.

'Let us in, let us in, we want to see the Goblin Dog and Fenella!' shouted Peter. 'The Goblin Dog is our friend! You shouldn't treat him like that!'

When the gatekeeper saw that it was Peter and Mary, he refused to open the gate.

'Don't you know that Lord Rolland said you were never to come into Fairyland again?' he said indignantly. 'Of course I shan't open the gate! You are two wicked children, and if the Goblin Dog is a friend of yours then you ought to be in prison too! Why, he had got our little Princess on his back and was flying right over Fairyland with her! If you don't go away at once I'll have you put into prison too!'

'Come away,' said Pop-Off to the two children. 'Something's gone wrong. Lord Rolland isn't going to forgive you, and he's punishing the poor old Goblin Dog, even though he helped us so. I expect Fenella has forgotten all about us.'

Very sadly the three of them walked away from the shining gates. It was dreadful to think that Fenella had forgotten them – but what else could they think? If she allowed the poor Goblin Dog to be thrown into prison she must indeed have forgotten her friends!

'Come home with us,' said Peter, slipping his arm through Pop-Off's. The pedlar was looking very sad. '*We* shan't forget how you've helped us, Pop-Off.'

They came to their own home at last. They pushed open the door and looked in. How lovely it was to be home once more! Their Mother was still lying in bed – and their father was cooking something in a pot by the fire. When they saw the two children they cried out in delight!

Peter and Mary flew to their mother and hugged her tightly, and then hugged their father. Pop-Off stood shyly by the door, feeling rather left out. But Mary took him by the hand and led him to their mother.

'Mother, this is Pop-Off, the pedlar,' she said. 'He has been such a good friend to us and to Fenella, and without him we should never have got home safely again.'

Their mother smiled at Pop-Off and held out her hand to him. She thanked him and told him that he would always be welcome at their cottage.

'We are poor,' she said, 'but you may know that what we have we will always share with you, Pop-Off.'

'But we're *not* poor now!' said Peter gleefully. He remembered the shining stones he had taken from the walls of the caves under the hill, and he emptied them out of his pocket on to the kitchen table. His father stared at them in amazement.

'They are worth a fortune!' he said. 'Tell me how you got them!'

Then all their adventures were told, Peter, Mary and Pop-Off talking fast, first one and then the other. Their father sat amazed, handling the precious stones in wonder. Their mother lay listening, frightened when she heard of all the dangers they had passed.

'Well, we rescued Fenella, as we said we would!' said Peter. 'And we've made Father rich with these shining stones. We shall be able to leave this little cottage and take a nice house, just as you have always wanted, Mother!'

'The only thing we haven't been able to do is to make Mother well,' said Mary.

'But *I* can do that!' said Pop-Off unexpectedly. He rummaged through his tray and found a small yellow bottle. 'This is witch-medicine, powerful enough to cure anyone of any illness. Take three doses, Madam, and you will be cured!'

Well what do you think of that? Peter and Mary could hardly believe their eyes! Their mother took a dose at once and said she felt better immediately.

'You will be able to get up after the second dose, and after the third you will be cured!' said Pop-Off, glad to think that he had been able to bring such happiness into the little family.

'I *am* hungry!' said Mary suddenly. 'It seems ages since we had tea in the little cave under the Shining Hill.'

'Well, there is supper in the larder,' said her mother. 'Lay the table, dear, and we'll all have supper together. Then you three must really go to bed, for you look tired out.'

So they all had a happy supper together, and Pop-Off said that the rabbit pie was the best he had ever tasted! Then he curled up with Peter

in his bed, and Mary went to hers. Soon they were fast asleep, and didn't even hear their parents talking about all the wonderful things they would do, as soon as they sold the shining stones.

The next morning was bright and shining. Away in the palace Fenella awoke in her own little white bed and wondered for a moment where she was. Then she remembered! How lovely, how lovely, she was at home again! She got up and danced round the room in delight. Then she stopped to remember what had happened the night before. Where was the Goblin Dog? Where were Peter, Mary and Pop-Off? What had happened to them?

'Oh, dear me, I was so tired last night that I must have fallen asleep without finding out what had happened to the dear old Goblin Dog and the others!' she thought in dismay. 'My goodness, what will they think of me? Oh, I do hope that the Dog has been made comfortable and his hurt wing bathed and bandaged!'

She ran to ask her mother – and when she heard that the dog had been taken prisoner, and that Peter and Mary had been turned away from the gates, the little Princess was very unhappy. Tears poured down her cheeks, and she began to tell the story of all that had happened.

'They are my best friends,' she sobbed. 'Peter and Mary rescued me, and the Goblin Dog was so kind and helpful. Oh, you shouldn't have put him in prison. He will be so unhappy!'

When her mother and father heard all that had happened, they were filled with astonishment. So Peter and Mary had *really* gone to rescue their little daughter – and the Goblin Dog was not wicked, but good and brave!

'This must be seen to,' said Lord Rolland at

once. 'We will get the Goblin Dog here and thank him.'

So, much to the Dog's surprise, he was taken from the prison to the palace – and there Fenella met him and flung her arms around his hairy neck. Lord Rolland and Lady Rozabel patted him and praised him, and very soon the court doctor had bound up his wing. He was given an enormous meal, and felt very happy indeed.

'And now, Mother and Father,' said Fenella

firmly, 'I want to ride on the Dog's back to Peter's home, and fetch him and Mary and Pop-Off back into Fairyland. And we are going to ride round all the streets so that the people can see us!'

Off she went, and soon the Goblin Dog arrived at the cottage in the valley. How delighted Peter, Mary and Pop-Off were to see him, and how they hugged Fenella!

'Jump on, all of you,' said the Princess beaming. 'We're all going back to Fairyland!'

'But will Peter and I be allowed in?' asked Mary doubtfully.

'Of course!' said Fenella. 'If they don't let you in, *I* won't go in either! I'll come and live with you!'

But, of course, they were all allowed in through the shining gates – and dear me, what a crowd of little folk there were, lining the streets and looking out of the windows to see them all pass by! How they cheered! You should have heard them!

'Three cheers for Fenella! Three cheers for Mary! Three cheers for Peter! Three cheers for Pop-Off! And three cheers for the good old Goblin Dog! Hip-hip-hurrah!'

Someone tied an enormous bow of red ribbon round the Goblin Dog's neck. He *was* so pleased! Then off to the palace they went and Fenella's father and mother helped them all off the Dog's broad back.

Lady Rozabel hugged Peter and Mary and thanked them very much for all they had done. She shook hands with Pop-Off, who blushed with pride.

'We'll have a big party in the palace garden this afternoon,' said Lord Rolland, smiling at everyone. 'Everybody shall come. And this evening we'll have fireworks!'

'Can the Goblin Dog sit next to me at tea-time?' asked Fenella anxiously. The Dog wagged his tail in the greatest delight.

'Of course!' said her father.

So that afternoon the Goblin Dog sat by Fenella, and Mary sat on her other side. Next to Mary and the Dog were Peter and Pop-Off, and next to Lady Rozabel and Lord Rolland were Peter's father and mother! Oh, it was a grand time!

'In return for the bravery and kindness of your children,' said Lord Rolland to Peter's father, 'I'm going to present you with a small castle not far from my palace, in Fairyland. And I shall hope that you will be good enough to allow your children to play with Fenella every day.'

155

Wasn't that lovely? How the children cheered!

'I shall be delighted to accept!' said Peter's father, bowing. He was very grand indeed in some fine clothes that he had bought with the money from the sale of the precious stones. 'I am a rich man now, thanks to the stones that Peter brought home, and I can well afford to live in a castle. My wife too, thanks to the pedlar's wonderful medicine, is quite cured of her illness.'

'Oh, Father, what about a reward for Pop-Off?' said Fenella. 'Could he come and live at the palace?'

'No, little Princess,' said Pop-Off, at once. 'I should not be happy living in one place. I am only happy when I am wandering about. But I will often come to visit you.'

'And we'll always buy all our ribbons, cottons, silks, tapes, buttons, hooksaneyes and everything from you!' said Fenella, hugging the blushing pedlar, who was really having the time of his life.

'What about the Goblin Dog? What shall his reward be?' asked Lady Rozabel, patting the happy Dog.

'*I'm* giving him his reward,' said Fenella, at once. 'I've already emptied my money-box, Mother, and I've given the money to Mister

Hammer, the pixie carpenter. He is making the Goblin Dog a most beautiful big kennel. And he's to live just outside my bedroom window and protect me all his life, because I love him so much!'

The Goblin Dog was so delighted that he cried big tears of joy into his dish of milk and biscuits. He couldn't ask for anything better than to look after the little Princess Fenella.

And now Peter and Mary live in their castle in Fairyland, and their mother and father are as grand as can be. They often see Pop-Off, and he always has tea with them and with Fenella when he visits them.

As for the Goblin Dog, you should see his kennel! It is painted a lovely blue, and every nail in it is made of gold. No wonder he is proud of it!

They all go for a ride on his broad back every Saturday afternoon for a treat, sitting between his great yellow wings – and you may be sure he *always* brings them back safe and sound!

THE FIRST GREEN GOBLIN BOOK

How Feefo, Tuppeny and Jinks Met Together

Once upon a time, on a hot sunny afternoon, a little green goblin sat on a stile and wept loudly. He was a small, round fellow, dressed in a green tunic, tight yellow stockings, pointed green shoes and a pointed green hat with a yellow feather in it. His eyes were as green as the grass, and his nose was like a round button.

'Hoo-hoo!' he wept. 'It's terrible, terrible!'

Across the field behind him there came another goblin, dressed just the same. He was tall and thin, and his nose was long and crooked. His eyes shone as green as seawater. When he heard the first goblin howling he stopped in surprise.

'What's the matter?' he asked, poking the crying goblin in the back.

'Ooh! Don't!' said the little fat creature, wriggling. 'I'm ticklish, and you'll make me laugh.'

'Well, laugh then!' said the tall goblin, poking him again.

'I don't want to,' said the other. 'I want to cry. Hoo-hoo-hoo!'

'Why?' asked the tall goblin.

'Well,' said the little one, 'I've been turned out of my cave in the Green Hills, where I lived with my friends. They said I was lazy and wouldn't do my share of the work, the mean things!'

'*Didn't* you work?' asked the tall goblin.

'Yes, very hard,' said the other, 'but not like they did. They dug all day in the dark cold caves, looking for gold and for precious stones. I liked the sunshine, so I used to go and dig in a little garden I had, to make flowers grow, and to listen to the birds singing. I didn't want to be rich. But I didn't want to be turned out of my nice little cave with its flowery garden outside!'

'Cheer up,' said the tall goblin, and he waggled his pointed ears to and fro, which made the little goblin begin to laugh. 'Let's seek our fortune together. What is your name? Mine is Feefo.'

'Mine's Tuppeny,' said the little fat one, drying his eyes. 'Will you really be my friend and let me come with you? Where are you going?'

'I don't know,' said Feefo, scratching his long nose. 'I left my hill of goblins because they laughed at my long nose and pointed ears. I thought I would go out into the world and make my fortune somehow. Can you do anything clever, Tuppeny?'

'I can sing. Listen!' said Tuppeny, proudly. He opened his mouth, blew out his chest and began to sing a loud song at the top of his voice.

'Very nice,' said Feefo, hastily. 'That'll do. My ears aren't very strong today.'

'Can *you* do anything clever?' asked Tuppeny, when he had got his breath.

'Not *very* clever,' said Feefo, modestly. 'I can just make noises.'

'Noises! *What* noises?' asked Tuppeny, in surprise.

'Oh, any noises,' said Feefo. 'You know – a railway train – or a cackling goose – or the wind in the chimney at night.'

'Jumping beetles!' cried Tuppeny, in amazement. 'Let's hear you! Make a noise like a railway train whistling in a tunnel.'

'PheeeEEEEEEEEEEeeeeeeeeee!' whistled Feefo, at once, and Tuppeny was so startled that he looked round to see if a railway train was anywhere near. Feefo was pleased.

'Now I'll make a noise like a lion and a bear fighting together,' he said. He shut his eyes, opened his mouth, worked his throat about like a bird's, and made such a truly terrible noise that Tuppeny fell off the stile in alarm and hid under the nearest bush, trembling.

When Feefo opened his eyes Tuppeny was nowhere to be seen, and he was most surprised.

'Where are you?' he called. 'Don't go away.'

Tuppeny crawled from under the bush, and dusted his tunic.

'What were you doing there?' asked Feefo, in astonishment.

'Just looking for mushrooms,' said Tuppeny. 'Don't make any more noises just now, Feefo. Let's walk on together and talk about how we can make our fortune.'

They left the stile and walked over the field. They hadn't gone far before they saw a very strange creature coming towards them. They

164

couldn't make it out at all. It had a large hat on, with a feather in it, but there didn't seem to be any face. The two goblins stopped in alarm.

'What is it?' said Tuppeny. 'I don't like it.'

'Nor do I,' said Feefo. 'Is it walking backwards, do you think? No, it can't be, because its boots are pointing this way. Ooh, what a strange creature!'

The creature came towards them, doing a little dance as it came. The hat wobbled on its head, and the goblins could *not* see any face however hard they looked.

When the creature was quite near it suddenly sprang upside down, landed on its 'head' and laughed loudly at the astonished faces of Feefo and Tuppeny.

'What's the matter?' asked the newcomer, grinning. 'Haven't you ever seen anyone walking on their hands before?'

'Oh – was *that* it?' said Feefo. 'But why did you put your hat on your feet? It made you look horrid, without any face, you know.'

'Well, if I put my hat on my head when I'm upside down, it falls off, silly!' grinned the goblin. 'Who are you? I'm Jinks.'

'This is Feefo and I'm Tuppeny,' said Tuppeny, who liked the look of the smiling goblin they had met. He was truly a strange-looking fellow, for his limbs seemed to be made of india-rubber, they were so long and supple. He had a cheerful, smiling face with a very pointed chin, and his eyes, like theirs, were a bright, shining green.

Jinks took his boots off his hands and put them on his feet. Then he solemnly shook hands with Feefo and Tuppeny and said he was pleased to meet them.

'I'm a pedlar,' he said, showing them a small basket on his back, which opened unexpectedly into quite a large tray. On it were the most extraordinary things – a tin kettle, a white mouse that seemed quite at home on the tray, a roll of green ribbon, one yellow shoe, half a loaf of bread, a red toothbrush, and many other things. 'Do you want to buy anything?'

'No, thank you,' said Feefo, at once. 'We haven't any money. We are seeking our fortunes.'

'It's no good seeking fortunes,' said Jinks, shutting up his tray with a snap into a small basket again. 'There's none to be found. *I* know that, because haven't I been seeking a fortune all over the country for years? And have I ever found the tail-end of one? Never!'

'Well, where are fortunes to be found then?' asked Tuppeny, dismally.

'I'll tell you!' said Jinks, dancing along beside them. 'I've an idea, and it's a grand idea, too. There's never been such an idea before!'

'Tell us about it!' begged Tuppeny and Feefo, beginning to feel excited, and dancing along too.

'Well, listen to this,' said Jinks, stopping and

banging his fist on his hand. 'If you want bread you go to a baker's, don't you? And if you want meat, you go to a butcher's. But suppose you want the tail-feather of a cockyolly bird to wear in your hat. Where would you get that? Or a handkerchief that will tie itself into knots whenever you want to remember anything. Where would you go for that? Aha! That's where *I* come in!'

Tuppeny and Feefo were excited but puzzled. How did Jinks come in?

'Go on!' they cried, and Feefo's ears waggled in excitement.

'Well, *I'm* going to buy a little shop and supply anything marvellous, strange or impossible that people want, whether they are fairies, witches, goblins or elves!' cried Jinks, turning a complete somersault. 'What do you think of that for an idea? What about *that* for making my fortune? Why, suppose a witch wanted a tiggle-taggle spell for making twisty magic with – she'd give a whole bag of gold to get it, wouldn't she! Then think how rich I'd be!'

'But – but – do you think you could get all these strange things that people might want?' asked Feefo, doubtfully.

'Ah, you don't know me!' said Jinks. 'I'm a clever chap, I am. All I want is a couple of friends to help me. What about you two?'

'Yes, we will!' said Feefo and Tuppeny at once, feeling pleased to think that a clever fellow like

167

Jinks should ask them. So off they all went together, talking nineteen to the dozen. Jinks sometimes walked on his hands and sometimes on his feet, and once or twice he joined his arms and legs together and rolled down a hill like a ball. You never knew what he was going to do next.

He was very pleased when he found that Feefo could make such extraordinary noises. He made him croak like a frog, cluck like three hens, snore like a hedgehog and rattle like twenty dustbin lids. It was really marvellous to hear Feefo. Then Tuppeny wanted to sing, but Jinks said he didn't

like singing, and every time poor Tuppeny started
he tickled him so that he laughed too much to go
on.

That night they slept under a hedge, and
cooked for breakfast some eggs and bacon that
Jinks had with him. They then walked on over the
fields and at last came to a pretty little village
called Heyho.

And it was there that Jinks saw the very cottage
he wanted for his fine new shop!

You should have seen it! It was a dear little
place with a thatched roof, a curly chimney and
a garden full of hollyhocks and sweet-williams,
pansies and white daisies, lavender and stocks. It
smelt sweet, it looked sweet and it *was* sweet!

'This shall be our cottage!' said Jinks, standing
by the gate. 'We'll move in at once.'

On the gate was the name – Hollyhock
Cottage. There was a big oblong window, made
of small diamond-shaped panes, along the front of
the cottage and Jinks said that they could put
their goods there for everyone to see.

Well, they moved in. They bought three tiny
beds, three small chairs and a little round table.
Jinks took a kettle from his basket, a saucepan
and a teapot. It was really a marvellous basket he
had – it seemed to be full of different things each
time, though the little white mouse was always
there.

The three goblins were soon very busy. They

169

painted the cottage white all over. They made a sign-board and on it they painted 'The Green Goblins'. They put some strange things in the

window, out of Jink's basket, and then Feefo printed a big notice to put in the window too. This is what he put –

WE SUPPPLY ANYTHING IN THE
WORLD FOR WITCHES, FAIRIES,
ELVES OR NOMES

Jinks said that 'supply' should only have one P,

and Tuppeny said it should have two. So Feefo put in one P for Jinks and two for Tuppeny to stop them quarrelling. Nobody knew that 'Nomes' was spelt wrong. It looked quite all right to them.

Then they waited for customers. They peeped behind the curtains in excitement and watched all the people come and read the notice in the window.

Three fairies came. Then a pixie ran up with tiny wings on her feet. Then an old witch hobbled up, using her magic broomstick as a walking stick. Then two gnomes with long beards reaching down to the ground.

They all read the notice, nodded their heads at one another, chattered about the new shop and went away. Nobody came in at all. It was most disappointing.

'I don't think much of your idea for making fortunes, Jinks,' said Tuppeny, gloomily, as he put the kettle on to make a cup of cocoa for supper.

Feefo made a noise like a hippopotamus with toothache and made Tuppeny jump so much that he dropped the kettle on to Jinks's toe. Jinks at once made a noise like Jinks being very angry and rushed at Tuppeny, who dodged behind the sofa in the corner.

'Oh! Ah! Ooh!' yelled Tuppeny, as Jinks pulled him out by the legs.

And then – and then – just as there was a

171

perfectly terrible noise going on, a big, deep voice came down the chimney and startled the three goblins almost out of their wits.

'HOO!' said the voice. 'HOO-HOO! I'm coming down the chimney! I'm the Windy Wizard and I'm sitting up on the roof. I want to come and buy something.'

'Don't come down the chimney!' called Jinks in a fright. 'There's a fire in the grate and you'll burn your toes. Come to the door.'

The Golden
Witch-bucket

But the Windy Wizard took no notice of Jinks.
He came down the chimney! First of all a great
draught blew down into the grate, and ashes went
flying all over the kitchen. The fire went out with
a strange pop and sizzle. Then two skinny bare
feet appeared down the chimney.

'Hi! Give me a tug!' called the Windy Wizard.
'Your chimney's small and I'm stuck.'

Jinks rushed forward and caught hold of the
wizard's legs. He pulled and the wizard came
down with a rush. He sat in the fireplace and
blinked at the three goblins. He was a very
strange fellow indeed.

He wore a gold suit that fitted him like a skin,
and over it a long cloak that flowed down to the
ground and was never still. It was black, set with
little twinkling stars. On his head was a tall,
pointed hat that kept slipping over one eye
because it was just a little too big. He wore a pair
of large green spectacles on his long nose.

'Don't you think you'd better get out of the

fireplace?' asked Feefo, anxiously. 'You blew the fire out, but I expect the coal is still hot.'

'It does feel a bit warm,' said the Windy Wizard, and he got up and came into the room.

'Ooh! Jumping beetles! You've burnt a big hole in your lovely cloak!' cried little Tuppeny, and he pointed to a large hole in the wizard's long cloak.

The wizard licked his thumb and passed it over the burn. In a trice the hole had disappeared and the cloak was as good as new.

'Won't you sit down?' asked Feefo, who was always the polite one. He pulled a chair out and the wizard sat down, his strange cloak swirling out round him. The three goblins shivered, for there seemed to be a wind in the room, and a very cold one it was for summertime.

'I saw your notice in the window,' said the wizard. 'I've come to order something from you – and if you get it for me I'll give you a sack full of golden pieces. Ha, what do you say to that?'

'Jumping beetles!' cried Tuppeny, in delight.

'*Sounds* all right,' said Feefo.

'But what have we got to *get* for you?' asked Jinks, cautiously.

'Oh, nothing much,' said the wizard, his cloak flapping in Jinks's face as if a wind was blowing it. 'I just want the Golden Bucket that belongs to old Witch Grumble. She stole it from me a hundred years ago, and now I want it back.'

'Oh, yes, I've heard the story,' said Jinks. 'But surely it isn't worth a whole sack of gold, Windy Wizard?'

'Ah, but it's a magic bucket!' said the wizard, his voice going down to a whisper. 'You know, whatever you throw into it disappears at once – such a useful way to get rid of rubbish. You've no idea what a lot of rubbish I have when I'm making spells, and there's no dustman where I live. My whole garden is piled with rubbish and I'm tired of it. If I could get my bucket back I could live tidily and pleasantly, for I could just throw anything I didn't want into the bucket and it would be gone for ever!'

'But where does the Grumble Witch live?' asked Feefo.

'She lives on a hill in the middle of the Dancing Sea,' said the wizard. 'And pray be careful of her, for she has a very nasty temper. I should be sorry to hear you had been turned into beetles, because you look nice little fellows.'

'J-j-j-jumping b-b-b-beetles!' said Tuppeny, in a fright.

'No, not jumping beetles, just ordinary beetles,' said the wizard. 'Well, I must go. Let me know when you have the Golden Witch-bucket, and I'll bring you your reward.'

He stood up and a draught whistled through the room again, making the goblins feel very cold. The black cloak wrapped itself tightly round the wizard, the candle went out, and when the goblins had lighted it again the Windy Wizard was gone! Goodness knows where he went to!

'Our first order!' said Jinks, rubbing his long hands together, pleased. 'We'll start off tomorrow.'

'I don't w-w-w-want to,' said poor Tuppeny, beginning to cry. He felt frightened.

'Don't be silly,' said Jinks, putting his arm round the fat little goblin. '*We*'ll look after you, Tuppeny. Cheer up! We are going to make our fortunes!'

They went to bed at once and blew out the candle. They awoke early, full of excitement. They shut up the shop, first putting a notice in the window, which said –

> GONE ON BIZNESS
> FOR OUR ONNERED
> CUSTUMER THE WINDY
> WIZZARD

Then Jinks slipped his pedlar's basket round his neck, in which he had put their toothbrushes, towels, a piece of soap, and some clean pairs of stockings. The little white mouse was excited to see the soap, and Tuppeny was afraid it might eat it. But Jinks said it wouldn't.

Then they slammed the door of Hollyhock Cottage and set off together, Tuppeny singing a very loud song indeed, and Feefo making a noise like a motorcar gone wrong. Jinks turned head-over-heels a few times, so it was no wonder that Heyho Village looked out of their windows in wonder at the three happy goblins.

'How do we get to the Dancing Sea?' asked Tuppeny

'I've looked it up on a map,' said Jinks. 'If we take the bus to Breezy Corner, we can get a boat there on the Rushing River. It goes down to the Dancing Sea. We are sure to be able to see the Witch's Hill then.'

'How shall we get the bucket from her?' asked Tuppeny.

'Oh, we don't need to think of that till we get there!' said Jinks, impatiently.

The bus was coming down the lane and the goblins hopped on to it. It was crowded with rabbits going to the Lettuce and Carrot Market in the next village. They were very hot to sit next to on a warm summer's day. Fat little Tuppeny began to puff and blow, and the rabbits next to him looked at him crossly.

'Will you please stop blowing my whiskers about?' said one, sternly. 'If you don't, I shall complain to the conductor.'

Tuppeny made himself as small as possible, blushed very red, and tried not to puff and blow. Jinks laughed loudly, and Feefo began to make a noise like seven dogs growling, barking and yelping. With one accord the rabbits rose up and fled from the bus.

'Where are those dogs?' asked the conductor, peering into the bus. 'If you've brought dogs with you, you must buy dog-tickets. Anyway, you ought to know better than to bring dogs into a bus where there are rabbit passengers.'

The three goblins looked innocent, and Jinks got up and looked under the seat for the dogs that he knew weren't there. That made Tuppeny giggle, and the conductor looked sternly at the goblins and said they had better behave themselves or he wouldn't have them in his bus.

After that they sat quietly, and very soon they came to Breezy Corner. The conductor didn't need to call out the name, for it was so windy that the bus nearly blew over! The three goblins tumbled out and looked for the Rushing River.

'There it is, over there!' cried Tuppeny, and they all set off as fast as they could go. There were many little boats tethered to the bank, but none had any oars.

'You don't need oars on this river,' said the pixie in charge of them. 'The river runs so fast that it takes you along without oars. You can't go *up* the river because the current is too strong.'

'But how do the boats come back to you?' asked Jinks, in astonishment.

'Oh, I keep a flock of swans and they bring all my boats back once a day,' said the pixie. He pointed to a swan swimming strongly up the Rushing River. It pulled a little boat behind it quite easily.

The goblins got into a boat and the pixie set it loose. It bounced off into the current and the three goblins held on tightly! Jinks guided the boat as best he could and shouted to Tuppeny not to lean over the side, or he might fall in. Tuppeny took no notice and Feefo just grabbed him in time

179

to save him from falling head-over-heels in the water. The boat rocked dangerously and everyone got splashed.

'You silly, stupid goblin!' shouted Jinks, in a temper. 'I've a good mind to leave you behind if you don't do as you're told!'

Tuppeny opened his mouth and howled in despair at being talked to like that. So Feefo put his arm round him and comforted him, though Jinks frowned for about five minutes and nearly

guided them into the bank. Then they all forgot their troubles and began to look for the Dancing Sea.

The river became wider and wider, and at last flowed into a bright blue sea. It was a strange sea, for, although there were no waves that broke, little dancing ripples and lines of white foam jigged up and down all the time. The boat jigged too, and Feefo turned green. He didn't like it at all!

'I shall be seasick!' he groaned.

'Oh, no, you won't!' said Jinks, at once, and he opened his wonderful basket. It spread out like a tray and Tuppeny saw the white mouse nibbling at their soap.

'There! I told you that mouse would eat our soap!' he cried. 'I shall put it into my pocket!'

He took the soap away and slipped it into his green tunic pocket. The mouse squeaked at him angrily and ran inside a green shoe that was on the tray. Jinks picked up a little green packet and shook out a pill, which he gave to poor, green-faced Feefo.

'Swallow that, and you'll be all right.' he said.

Feefo swallowed it, and then, to everyone's surprise and alarm, he immediately began to grow twice as large as he had been, and the boat rocked dangerously.

'Ooh! I've given him the wrong pill!' said Jinks, in fright. 'Quick, Feefo, swallow this one instead!'

Poor Feefo swallowed it, and to Jinks's and Tuppeny's relief he went back to his own size again.

181

'Now I feel more seasick than ever,' said the poor goblin, holding his head in his hand. His long, pointed ears drooped down like a rabbit's, and Tuppeny felt very sorry for him.

Jinks scrabbled about on his tray and at last found some more green pills. He gave one to Feefo, and as it really was the right one this time Feefo soon cheered up and felt better.

Then Jinks took a look round to see where they were. Dear me, they were quite out of sight of land! The blue sea lay all round them, dancing up and down in the sunshine, jigging into little points, rippling gaily.

'Where are we?' cried Tuppeny, in alarm.

'Where do you suppose?' said Jinks. 'Sitting on someone's chimney-top?'

Feefo giggled, but Tuppeny frowned. He didn't like being laughed at. He looked all round him and then he suddenly gave a loud shout.

'See! There's the Witch's Hill!'

The others looked. Sure enough, far away on the horizon, a steep hill rose up out of the sea. It looked rather small to the three goblins because they were far away, but as they drew nearer they saw that it was really a very big hill indeed.

At last the boat grated on the shingly beach of the island hill. The three goblins jumped out and looked at the castle that stood high up on the top. A long, long flight of steps led up to it.

'Ooh dear!' said fat little Tuppeny, when he

saw all those steps. 'I shall never get up to the top!'

'Well, you've got to!' said Jinks. 'Because *you're* going to get the Golden Witch-bucket!'

'*Me!*' cried Tuppeny, in alarm. 'Oh, I couldn't!'

'Now, just listen to my plan,' said Jinks, and they all sat down on the beach. 'It's perfectly simple. In fact, it's a plan that's been used before very successfully. Do you remember in the story of Aladdin how the magician there got back the magic lamp?'

'Yes, he went round shouting "New Lamps for Old!" ' said Feefo, at once. 'And he got the old magic lamp back in return for a new one that wasn't magic.'

'Yes,' said Jinks. 'Well, that's what I thought

we'd do. I'll get a nice new pail out of my basket and Tuppeny shall take it up to the castle and offer it to the servants there in return for any old one they have. Then perhaps they'll give him the Witch-bucket!'

'And perhaps they won't!' said Feefo.

'I'm not going to go up to the castle alone,' said Tuppeny, firmly. 'If your plan is so good, Jinks, you'd better do it yourself. I shall only make a muddle of it.'

'No, I chose you because you look such a nice, fat, jolly little fellow,' said Jinks. 'Nobody would ever think you would play a clever trick on them. Go on, Tuppeny, just try. We will come up the steps with you, and we'll hide somewhere and watch what happens. You won't be alone.'

'All right,' said Tuppeny. 'But if anything happens to me, promise me something, both of you – save me somehow, won't you?'

'Of course,' said Jinks and Feefo together, and they hugged the fat, solemn little goblin.

Then they began to climb up the steps to the witch's castle. Oh, what a long way! How they panted and puffed, how they sighed and grumbled!

At last they reached the top. In front of them was the castle yard, and the back door stood wide open. A great noise of chattering came out from it, and clouds of steam rushed out of the door.

'Washing day!' whispered Jinks to the others.

'That means there will be lots of pails used and perhaps the servants will be pleased to have a new one from Tuppeny, in exchange for the old Witch-bucket. It must be very old and dirty now.'

Jinks opened his basket and made it into a tray. In the very middle stood a marvellous, shining, new bucket!

'Jumping beetles!' said Tuppeny, in surprise. 'Look at that!'

'Look at that!'

Jinks gave the bucket to Tuppeny and pushed him towards the kitchen door of the castle. 'Go on!' he said. 'Do your best.'

Rather shaky at the knees, poor little Tuppeny marched over to the kitchen door. The others heard him shout in his high voice.

'New buckets for old! New buckets for old!'

A fat and untidy cook came to the door. She looked kindly at little Tuppeny and smiled at him.

'Well, my little man,' she said. 'So you've come to our castle, have you? What's that you've got? A fine new bucket?'

'Yes, and you can have it for an old one,' said Tuppeny.

'That's funny!' said the cook, looking hard at Tuppeny. He felt uncomfortable. Perhaps it did sound strange to offer a new bucket for an old one.

'Well, you can give me a good meal too, if

you like,' he said, smiling up at the kindly faced cook.

'Ah, I thought you'd want something else, too!' she said, patting him on the shoulder. 'Well, wait a minute, mannikin, and you shall have a fine dinner. I'll set you a little table in the yard here, for the scullery and kitchen are full of steam. I can do with a new bucket today. My old one has a leak in it.'

She took the shining new bucket from Tuppeny, and gave him an old, rusty one, with a hole in the bottom. Jinks and Feefo, who were watching from behind a tree, were simply delighted to see how easily their plan had worked. They expected Tuppeny to come rushing over to them – but he didn't.

Instead he sat himself down at a little table the cook brought out and then, to the other goblins' envy and disgust, the fat little fellow set to work to eat a lovely dinner that the cook set before him.

She gave him four fried sausages, a large potato, six fried tomatoes and a great deal of gravy. For his pudding he had a piece of suet with a great lake of golden treacle round it.

Jinks and Feefo, who had had nothing to eat since they left home, were very jealous. They sniffed the good dinner, and each of them wished he had gone to the kitchen door instead of Tuppeny. That little goblin turned round and beamed in triumph at them. The old bucket stood beside him, and Jinks longed to get hold of it. Suppose anything happened to it before Tuppeny came to them? Suppose the old witch came out and saw it?

But nothing at all happened to the old bucket. It just stood there whilst Tuppeny ate his dinner.

Poor Little Tuppeny

When Tuppeny had finished his dinner he took his plates to a pump in the yard and carefully washed them. Then he went to the kitchen door and called to the cook. The servants were having their dinner and at first they did not hear Tuppeny's voice. So he walked into the scullery and looked round.

The the cook saw him and hustled him out. 'No one's allowed to come inside!' she cried. 'Shoo, little mannikin, shoo!'

Tuppeny was frightened. He gave the cook the plates and fled, taking the rusty old bucket with him. As soon as he reached Feefo and Jinks they took the bucket from him in delight.

'You were lucky to get a good meal like that,' said Jinks, enviously.

'Well, I earned it!' said Tuppeny. 'Wasn't I clever and brave enough to go and get the Witch-bucket for you? I deserved a good meal.'

'Let's throw some rubbish into the bucket and see it disappear,' said Jinks, who was longing to try the Witch-bucket's strange powers. So Feefo picked up a paper bag that was blowing round the yard and some twigs from under a tree. He threw them all into the bucket and the three goblins bent over it excitedly to see them vanish out of sight.

But they didn't! No, they just stayed in the bucket and didn't go away at all. Jinks put in his hand and stirred the rubbish round a bit. No good at all! It just stayed there all the same.

'Jumping beetles!' said Tuppeny. 'It can't be the right bucket!'

The three sat down and looked at one another in dismay. What a terrible shock!

Then Tuppeny had an idea and he jumped to his feet in excitement.

'Of course! I *saw* the right bucket when I went into the scullery just now! It must be the one. It was hanging on a nail over the sink, and it was shining like gold. Why should we think the Witch-bucket ought to be old and dirty? It is much more likely to be well polished and shining bright!'

'Ooh!' said Jinks and Feefo at once, their faces brightening. 'Ooh! Then, Tuppeny, you could perhaps just go across and get the bucket?'

'Why shouldn't *you*?' demanded Tuppeny, fiercely. 'I've had my turn.'

'Yes – but you know where the bucket is and we don't,' said Jinks at once.

'All right, all right,' said Tuppeny, sighing. 'I'll go – but if I get caught, remember what you promised, you two. You said you would rescue me.'

'Of course,' said Jinks and Feefo, together. 'Go on, now, Tuppeny, whilst the servants are having dinner in the kitchen.'

So Tuppeny crept softly across the yard again and peeped in at the scullery. No servants were there. It was quite empty. He tiptoed inside, went to the sink and unhooked the shining bucket from its nail. Then he turned to run.

But poor little Tuppeny tripped over a mat and down he went, the bucket clanging behind him on the floor! Oh dear!

A loud and angry voice came from the kitchen and someone ran to the scullery. It was the Grumble Witch herself, followed by all the surprised servants. Tuppeny gave a screech when he saw the green-eyed witch and ran for his life, taking the bucket with him.

The witch ran after him, shouting and roaring in rage.

'Bring me back my bucket, you wicked little goblin!'

'It isn't yours, it belongs to the Windy Wizard!' yelled Tuppeny.

Jinks and Feefo, when they saw the old witch pounding along, her bright red dress flying out behind her, were full of alarm. They rushed to the

castle steps and ran down them as quickly as ever
they could. They were soon at the bottom and
they looked up, hoping that Tuppeny would join
them, then they could run and hide.

Tuppeny was tearing down the steep steps as
fast as his fat little legs could carry him. Suddenly
he slipped and dropped the bucket, which went
clanging and bumping down the steps to the very
bottom, where it stood upright. Tuppeny rolled
over and over too, and at last reached the bottom
– but oh my goodness gracious, what *do* you suppose happened? Why, Tuppeny fell straight into
the big Witch-bucket – and, of course, as it

really *was* the magic bucket this time, he disappeared!

Jinks, thinking that Tuppeny was inside the bucket, caught it up and ran off with it, Feefo beside him. They ran to the boat they had left on the beach, and, what a pleasant surprise! A big white swan was there, too, waiting to take the boat back to the pixie on the Rushing River!

The two goblins tumbled into the boat and the swan at once swam off quickly. The witch stood on the shore and shook her fist at them. Then she suddenly cried out a strange magic spell, and to the goblins' great alarm, the sea began to heave up enormous waves and toss the little boat about like a cork.

'This isn't a *Dancing* Sea, this is a Jumping and Skipping Sea!' groaned poor Feefo, who was feeling very seasick again. 'I say, Jinks, we shall be wrecked!'

But the swan saved them. It didn't like the choppy sea, so it suddenly spread its great white wings and flew up into the air, taking the boat with it on a rope!

Jinks and Feefo nearly fell out! Jinks clutched the side of the boat and the bucket just in time. Feefo clung on with both hands and stopped feeling seasick. The witch could do nothing more, and they saw her climbing up the steep steps to her castle.

'Get Tuppeny out of the bucket,' said Feefo to
Jinks. 'He'll be more comfortable in the boat.'

Jinks looked into the big bucket and spoke.

'Hallo, there, Tuppeny, come out! You're safe
now.'

But, of course, there was no Tuppeny there!
The bucket was empty. Jinks gave a scream and
turned pale.

'What's the matter?' asked Feefo, scared.

'Tuppeny's gone!' said Jinks, tears coming into
his eyes.

193

'*Gone!* What do you mean, *gone*?' said Feefo.

'Just gone,' said Jinks, wiping his eyes. 'Oh, Feefo, don't you see what has happened? This is the magic bucket, and when Tuppeny tumbled into it he went the way of any rubbish that is put in. He disappeared!'

Feefo was so horrified that his hair stood straight up from his head and his hat fell off into the boat. He couldn't say a word. But tears poured down his thin cheeks, for he was very fond of little fat Tuppeny.

'W-w-w-w-what shall we d-d-d-do?' sniffed Jinks. 'How can we get T-t-t-tuppeny back?'

'We promised to save him if anything ever happened to him,' said Feefo, finding his voice at last.

'Perhaps the Windy Wizard can tell us how to save him,' said Jinks, drying his eyes. 'Do you mind turning the other way if you want to cry any more, Feefo? Your tears are making a puddle round my feet.'

'Sorry,' said Feefo, feeling about for his handkerchief. 'Oh, Jinks, this is terrible. Poor little Tuppeny! To think we made him get the bucket for us! It's all our fault!'

'Well, we'll ask the Windy Wizard to help us,' said Jinks. 'He's sure to know where Tuppeny has gone. Then when we know we'll go and rescue him.

The swan flew on and on over the stormy sea. When it reached the Rushing River it flew down to the water again and the boat flopped on to the river. Then very swiftly the swan swam up the river until it reached the place where the little pixie kept his boats.

Jinks and Feefo jumped out, paid the pixie and hurried off to catch the bus back to Heyho Village. It was full of rabbits again, this time going back from the Lettuce and Carrot Market, but the two goblins felt so sad that they played no tricks at all. They sat quietly in a corner, sometimes sniffing sadly when they thought of poor little Tuppeny.

They got out at Hollyhock Cottage and went sorrowfully up the path. Then Jinks wrote a letter to the Windy Wizard and told him he had got the magic Witch-bucket and please would he call and fetch it.

That night the wizard came. Once more he came down the chimney and blew the fire out. He looked all round the kitchen very eagerly for his bucket, but he couldn't see it. In his hand he carried a small sack which chinked when he put it down. But even the sound of so many gold pieces couldn't make Jinks and Feefo smile.

'Great elephants! What's the matter with you?' asked the wizard in amazement. 'Are you bewitched?'

'No, but poor Tuppeny is!' said Jinks; and he told the Windy Wizard all that had happened.

'Well, I can't help that,' said the wizard,

impatiently. 'That bucket is all I care about. It's your own carelessness that lost you your companion. Give me the bucket and take your pay.'

'We want you to tell us where Tuppeny is,' said Jinks, firmly. 'We've got to rescue him.'

'I can't waste my time chattering to you,' said the wizard, his black, twinkling cloak swirling out round him as if it were impatient. 'Give me my bucket and let me go.'

'No, you shan't have the bucket until you tell us where Tuppeny is,' said Feefo and Jinks both together.

'Well, he's gone where all the rubbish goes,' said the wizard.

'Where's that?' asked Jinks, in dismay.

'In the great caves of the Hoo-Moo-Loos,' said the wizard, wrapping his cloak tightly round him. 'You'll have to go to the end of the rainbow, find a toadstool with six red spots underneath and let it take you down to the caves. The King is an odd chap called Tick-Tock because he loves to have hundreds of clocks all round him. He may want to keep you prisoner if you go there, so be careful. Now where's that bucket?'

Jinks took it from a cupboard and placed it in front of the delighted wizard. He danced round it and clapped his hands for joy. It stood there, big and shining, made of pure gold.

'Give me some paper and let me see if the magic is still in it,' said the wizard.

'Well, of course it's still magic,' cried Jinks, impatiently. 'How do you suppose Tuppeny disappeared if the bucket isn't magic?'

But the wizard wanted to make certain. So Feefo and Jinks took an old newspaper and crammed it into the bucket. It vanished at once! Then they emptied the tea leaves out of their teapot. Those disappeared too. Then Jinks, in a moment of mischief, seized the end of the wizard's long cloak and stuffed that into the bucket as well. The wizard gave a yell and tugged it out again at once, before it had had time to disappear.

'Stupid, silly creature!' he cried, and gave Jinks a box on the ear. 'I've a good mind to put *you* in!'

'Sorry,' said Jinks, half-frightened. 'Take your bucket, wizard, and leave us the gold.'

The wizard picked up the bucket, blew out the candle on the table and disappeared in a swirl of black cloak. Jinks and Feefo couldn't make out if he had gone through the door, jumped out of the window or flown up the chimney. He was really a very strange visitor.

The two goblins undid the sack. It was full of shining gold pieces!

'There's a fortune for you!' cried Jinks. But Feefo shook his head sadly.

'What's the good of a fortune if you lose a good friend? Put the gold away in a cupboard, Jinks, and let us think of Tuppeny instead. The very

next time we see a rainbow we must set off to find the end of it.'

So the gold was put away, and the two sad little goblins undressed themselves and got into bed, after having a cup of very hot cocoa and two pieces of brown bread and butter each.

'Good night, Jinks,' said Feefo.

'Good night, Feefo,' said Jinks. 'I do wonder what poor little Tuppeny is doing, don't you?'

The Land of the
Hoo-Moo-Loos

The next day was fine with never a spot of rain.
The day after was fine, too, but in the morning
a raincloud blew up and a shower fell. At the same
time the sun shone and a lovely rainbow glowed
from the clouds to the earth.

'Look! Quick!' cried Jinks, and ran out into
the garden. 'See, Feefo! The end of the rainbow
is touching the Tiptop Hill over there. Can you
see?'

'Yes,' said Feefo, screwing up his eyes. 'It is just
touching that gorse-bush, I think. Come on,
Jinks, put on your basket and your hat and we'll
go. There might not be another rainbow for
weeks, and we must rescue Tuppeny as soon as
ever we can. He will be very unhappy all by
himself in a strange country.'

Off they went across the fields towards Tiptop
Hill. This was a fairly steep hill, covered with
gorse and bracken. The goblins toiled up it to the
gorse-bush that they had thought was touched by
the end of the rainbow. The rainbow had long

199

since vanished, of course, but the gorse-bush was still there.

They came to it at last. 'Now we must hunt for a toadstool with six red spots underneath,' said Feefo. So they searched all round and about. But there was no toadstool at all.

'Perhaps it's under the gorse-bush,' said Jinks, at last.

'Ooh! I hope not!' said Feefo. 'It's so prickly!'

But that's just where it was! Jinks crawled right underneath and gave a shout.

'It's here – quite a large one. My, it's prickly under this bush. Be careful, Feefo, or you'll be scratched to bits!'

Feefo crawled under, groaning. He saw the toadstool at once and looked underneath it. Sure enough, it had six red spots.

'I suppose we sit on it and wish to be taken to the Land of the Hoo-Moo-Loos,' said Jinks. There was hardly room to squeeze himself on to the toadstool, but he and Feefo managed somehow. Then Jinks wished.

WhhhhooooooOOOOOOOOOOOOSH!

What a surprise for the goblins! The toadstool sank downwards at a terrific speed, taking their breath away! They clung tightly to it, afraid of tumbling off. They couldn't possibly see what they were passing for the toadstool went far too quickly.

'It's a sort of lift,' shouted Jinks to Feefo. The

toadstool was making such a loud whooshing noise that he had to shout.

Ker-plunk! The toadstool came to a sudden stop and the goblins bounced off at once.

'Ooh!' said Jinks, rubbing his bruised leg.

'Ow!' groaned Feefo, feeling his arms to see if they were broken.

'Tickets, please,' said a booming voice and a very large mole, dressed like a ticket-collector, came out of the darkness towards them. They were far underground and the cave they were in was lighted by one green lamp swinging from the roof.

'Tickets!' said Jinks, indignantly. 'What do you mean, tickets! We haven't any!'

'You ought to have tickets if you use our lift,' said the mole severely, waving his spade-like paws about. 'Everybody does. You'd better come with me.'

Now Jinks certainly didn't want to be marched off and locked up anywhere so he racked his brains to think what to do. Then a bright idea came to him.

'Feefo!' he whispered. 'If there's one thing that moles like more than another, it's worms. Can you make a noise like a dozen worms having a tea-party, do you think?'

'Easy!' said Feefo, and at once a most curious sound filled the cave. It made you think of wrigglings, squirmings and writhings, and the mole at once began to twitch his sensitive nose.

'Worms!' he muttered. 'Where are they? A whole lot of them by the sound! But I can't smell them! Ooh, worms, worms!'

He rushed off into a corner and began to dig violently, forgetting all about Jinks and Feefo, who were giggling softly together. 'Come on,' whispered Feefo. 'He's safe for a few minutes!'

So they stole off into another cave, hearing an excited mutter behind them in the dark corner of the cave, of 'Worms, wor-r-rums, worms!'

The two goblins went through cave after cave. Some were dark, some were lighter. Some were enormous, some were very small, so small that Feefo and Jinks had to duck their heads when walking through them.

At last they met one of the Hoo-Moo-Loos. He was the funniest little chap they had ever seen in their lives. At first the goblins didn't think he was alive. They thought he was a big ball, rolling along!

That is just what he looked like as he came towards them – but as soon as he came up to them, a head sprang out of the ball, and two arms

and two legs jerked out as if they were on springs
– and hey-presto, there was the Hoo-Moo-Loo,
with the roundest, fattest body, and funny little
head, arms and legs!

'Goodness!' said Jinks, in astonishment. 'How
do you do it?'

'Do what?' asked the Hoo-Moo-Loo in a rich,
juicy sort of voice.

'Well, roll along like that?' said Jinks.

'How *do* I?' said the Hoo-Moo-Loo, in surprise.
'Well I might say to you – how *don't* you! It's
much easier to roll than walk.'

'H'm, that depends,' said Jinks. 'Tell me,
is this the land where all the rubbish comes
to?'

'Yes,' said the Hoo-Moo-Loo. 'And do you
know, such a strange piece of rubbish arrived the
other day. It was a little fat, green goblin!'

Jinks and Feefo looked at one another in
delight.

'What's happened to him?' asked Jinks.

'Oh, he was locked up in the Rubbish Cave
because he was rude to King Tick-Tock,' said the
Hoo-Moo-Loo.

'Poor Tuppeny!' said Jinks. 'Where is the
Rubbish Cave?'

'Aha! Wouldn't you like to know!' said the
strange little creature, grinning. He suddenly
shot his head in, jerked his arms and legs into his
ball-like body and became a round, rolling thing

that shot away between Jinks's legs and nearly sent him tumbling to the ground.

'Rude creature!' said Jinks, crossly. They watched the Hoo-Moo-Loo roll away into the darkness.

'Well, it's something to know that Tuppeny is here!' said Feefo, gladly, and he made a noise like six canaries singing loudly.

'What's that, what's that?' suddenly cried dozens of rich, juicy voices, and into the cave rolled about fifty round Hoo-Moo-Loos of all sizes. Some were no bigger than large apples, some were bigger than the goblins themselves. They all shot up heads, and jerked out arms and legs so that in a trice the cave was filled with the funny Hoo-Moo-Loos.

Jinks and Feefo were surrounded by them, and were dragged along to a much larger cave. This was a very strange place, full of ticking, chiming and striking. It was lighted by great lamps set in the walls, and when the two goblins looked round they could see hundreds and hundreds of clocks set on shelves around the cave. At the end of the cave was a throne and on it sat the biggest Hoo-Moo-Loo of all, holding a wrist-watch to his ear to hear it tick.

He wore a crown on his head set with tiny golden watches. It looked very strange.

'He must be mad on clocks!' whispered Jinks to Feefo.

'Silence!' roared the King. 'Who dares to speak when I listen to my new wristwatch ticking?'

Jinks was just going to say something when every clock in the cave began to chime twelve o'clock at once. The King forgot to frown and listened with a pleased smile. But suddenly he sighed and shook his head. He pointed to a large clock on the wall near Feefo and said, 'I suppose you can't tell me how to wind up that clock, goblin?'

Feefo looked at the clock. There was no key-hole anywhere, so it was quite impossible to wind it up. Just as he was about to answer, Jinks gave him a poke in the ribs with his elbow.

'Your Majesty,' said Jinks, breathlessly, 'my friend, Feefo, is marvellous at winding clocks. He can wind this clock up for you, if you like – but you must in return do something for him.'

'Anything, anything!' cried the King, delighted.

'But, Jinks, I can't w –' Feefo began to whisper to Jinks, who gave him another nudge and frowned so fiercely at him that he said no more. Whatever could Jinks be thinking of?

'Well, if you will set free the little green goblin who came here the other day as rubbish, my friend will wind up your clock for you,' said Jinks.

'Will it go if he winds it up?' asked the King.

'That I can't tell you,' said Jinks. 'You can sit by it and wait for it to tick after it has been wound up, if you like. That would be interesting for you.'

'Wind it up, then,' commanded the round, fat King.

'Tell us where the other goblin is, first,' said Jinks.

'He's in the Rubbish Cave, of course,' said the King, impatiently. 'I'll tell one of the Hoo-Moo-Loos to take you there as soon as the clock is wound up. And just you tell that goblin not to be rude to kings next time. He called me a jumping beetle!'

'Oh, but that's just something he says when he's surprised or frightened,' said Feefo.

'Don't argue,' said the King. 'Wind up my clock at once.'

'Go on, Feefo,' said Jinks. But Feefo just stood miserably there, and didn't do anything. 'You silly creature, can't you pretend to take a key out of your pocket and then make a noise like a clock being wound up?' whispered Jinks, fiercely. Feefo's face cleared up at once and he grinned delightedly. Make a noise like a clock being wound up? Ho, that was easy!

He walked over to the clock, and pretended to take a key out of his pocket. It was really only a nail he had there. He pretended to push it into an imaginary keyhole, and then, dear me, bless us all, you should have heard that clock being wound up!

Feefo made a most marvellous noise – a harsh, grating, rusty sort of noise for all the world like a clock being wound up when it has been unwound for hundreds of years. Jinks jumped up and down in delight. How clever Feefo was!

'There you are!' said Feefo, at last, turning to the King, who was listening closely. 'Now if you bring your throne over here and listen for a little while perhaps your old clock will begin to tick. It may have forgotten how to, so you must tap it now and again just to encourage it.'

'A thousand thanks!' said the Hoo-Moo-Loo King, gratefully. 'Hi, Runaround! Take these goblins to the Rubbish Cave and set the other goblin there free.'

A small Hoo-Moo-Loo came up. He shot in his arms and legs and his head too, and rolled away in front of the two goblins. They followed quickly, looking round as they left the cave, to see the King dragging his throne over to his precious clock!

'You did that well,' whispered Jinks, squeezing Feefo's hand.

Through many caves and dark passages they hurried and at last came to one with a large wooden door, set with huge nails that gleamed like lamps. A loud voice came from behind the door, singing a song.

> 'I certainly would never choose
> To make a friend of Hoo-Moo-Loos,
> No, no, no!
> Each one is just a rolling ball,
> I do not like the Hoos at all,
> No, no, NO!'

'That's Tuppeny!' said Jinks, in delight. 'I'd know his enormous voice anywhere! What a cheeky song he's singing!'

The Hoo-Moo-Loo with them stood up on his

legs, jerked out his arms and head and unbolted the door. Jinks and Feefo rushed into the Rubbish Cave – and there was fat little Tuppeny, sitting on a pile of rubbish, singing with all his might, while tears poured down his fat cheeks!

'Jinks! Feefo!' he cried, in amazement. 'Is it really you? Oh, how lovely! Oh, you don't know how unhappy I've been! Oh, it was dreadful to tumble into that Witch-bucket and find myself falling into the horrid caves of the Hoo-Moo-Loos!'

'Dear Tuppeny!' said the others, hugging him. 'But you sounded very jolly, singing like that.'

'Oh, that was just to keep my spirits up,' said Tuppeny, wiping his eyes happily. 'Look at this disgusting place they've put me in! They said I was rude to their fat old King, just because I was frightened and said "Jumping Beetles". This is the Rubbish Cave and all the rubbish of the world comes here, I should think!'

There were stacks of papers there, broken pots, bent tins and all kinds of things. As they looked, a heap of green feathers and some odd toadstools came flying down on their heads from the empty air.

'There you are!' said Tuppeny, taking the feathers out of his hat, where some of them had stuck. 'That's the sort of thing that *keeps* happening here!'

'I guess those feathers and toadstools are some of the rubbish that the Windy Wizard has been throwing into his magic bucket,' said Feefo. 'It looks like it!'

'Come on,' said Jinks. 'Don't let's wait here. When the King finds that that silly old clock doesn't go he may come and chase us.'

The three goblins hurried away from the Rubbish Cave, and took a passage that went to the right, away from the King's cave. But they hadn't

gone very far before there came the sound of rolling Hoo-Moo-Loos behind them, and the goblins stopped in alarm.

The Hoo-Moo-Loos jumped to their feet and one of them called to Feefo.

211

'Goblin! The King wants that key with which you wound up his clock! It has not ticked yet, and he thinks he will wind it up again.'

'I only used a nail,' whispered Feefo to Jinks, in despair. 'Now what are we to do?'

But Jinks was never at a loss. He opened his pedlar's basket at once and felt about in it. Tuppeny could hear the little white mouse squeaking as usual. Jinks found a key and handed it solemnly to the waiting Hoo-Moo-Loos. They took it, made themselves round again and rolled off.

'Quick!' said Jinks. 'They'll certainly be after us again when they find that the key won't wind!'

They hurried on together and at last came to a little cave in which grew a batch of small toadstools, just like the one on which they had come down to the caves.

'Good!' cried Jinks. 'If we sit on these and wish ourselves above ground, we'll be safe.'

Just as they were sitting on the toadstools six Hoo-Moo-Loos came rolling up, shouting, 'What have you done with the keyhole? It isn't there!'

'I wish that we were safely in the open air,' wished Jinks, quickly – and before the Hoo-Moo-Loos could do anything the three toadstools shot up through holes in the cave roof and rose swiftly until they darted out of the ground and came to a stop, sending the three goblins spinning!

'Now run!' cried Jinks, and they ran for their

lives – though they needn't have bothered, for there was nobody after them at all.

Soon they were at Hollyhock Cottage and how pleased Tuppeny was to see it again. He felt as if he had been away for years!'

'Look at all the gold that the Windy Wizard brought us for that Witch-bucket!' said Jinks, shaking out the pieces on the table. 'You shall have most of it, Tuppeny, because you got the bucket!'

'No, let's share alike,' said Tuppeny. 'You rescued me, so it's only fair. We'll all go and buy some new suits and have muffins and crumpets for tea, shall we?'

So out they went, arm-in-arm together, singing for all they were worth!

A Peculiar Adventure in Dreamland

For a week or two the goblins had a lovely time. They spent their money on all sorts of exciting things, especially things to eat. They bought themselves new green suits and new yellow stockings. They spent two gold pieces on a fine armchair and took it in turns to sit in it each night.

Nobody came to order anything from them for two weeks – and then they had their second customer. She came in at the shop door in quite an ordinary way and said 'Good afternoon' very politely.

Jinks got up to see what she wanted. He saw a fairy standing by the counter, dressed in a blue, frilly dress, with great silver wings behind her and the prettiest little face he had ever seen.

'Good afternoon! What can I do for you?' asked Jinks, delighted to see such a pretty visitor.

'Well, you say you can get anything in the world,' said the fairy. 'So I've come to ask you if you'll get me the longest feather out of the Blue

Bird's tail. He lives in Dreamland, you know, and he won't usually let anyone have any of his feathers, not even those that fall out. But I badly want one to stir some magic. The spell *won't* go right!'

'We'd get you *anything!*' said Jinks, smiling at the lovely fairy. 'When do you want it?'

'Oh, as soon as you can get it,' said the fairy. 'My name is Tiptoe and I live next door to you, in Cherry-Tree Cottage. I hope you'll come to tea with me one day.'

'We should be very pleased,' said Jinks. 'Hi, Tuppeny, hi, Feefo, come and be introduced to Fairy Tiptoe. She wants us to do something for her.

Tuppeny and Feefo came running into the shop and stopped in delight when they saw Tiptoe. They shook hands with her, and said yes, of course, they would get whatever she wanted.

'Do you know the best way to go to Dreamland?' asked Tiptoe.

'No, not really,' said Jinks. 'Do you?'

'Yes,' said Tiptoe. 'It is best to go there in your sleep, though some people will tell you that you can fly there by the Dreamland Aeroplane. But that is very expensive and sometimes takes you to Nightmare Land instead, which isn't at all nice.'

'Well, we'll go there in our sleep,' said Jinks. 'We'll go this very evening!'

'Thank you,' said Tiptoe, and ran back to her

215

own cottage, thinking what nice creatures the
three green goblins were.

After the goblins had had tea they got ready to
go to Dreamland. They all sat together in the big
armchair and Jinks hummed a little magic song to
send them to sleep. Presently their eyes closed
and Feefo snored very gently. They were asleep!

The armchair they were in began to rock about
on its four legs. It rocked to the door and pushed
it open. Then it suddenly grew great black wings
behind it and rose into the evening sky, flying
towards the setting sun. It was strange to see it.

216

The three goblins slept soundly. The armchair flew on and on and at last came to a land where the sun shone brightly through a misty haze that spread everywhere. This was Dreamland.

The armchair flew gently downwards and landed with a bump in a beautiful garden. The bump woke up the goblins and they sat up and rubbed their eyes. They were most astonished when they found that although they were still sitting in their armchair they were not in their cosy cottage!

'Jumping beetles!' said Tuppeny, of course, looking round. 'Where are we?'

'Well, I suppose it's Dreamland,' said Jinks. 'Come on – we must go and find the Blue Bird if we can.'

'But what about our armchair?' said Feefo. 'We can't leave it here.'

'Well, we must take it with us, then,' said Jinks. 'It's a nuisance, but we simply *can't* leave such a nice chair behind.'

So Jinks and Feefo picked up the big armchair and began to stagger along with it, Tuppeny holding on to one of the legs.

And then, as they went down the path in the garden, a most strange and peculiar thing happened! The armchair suddenly became less heavy and much softer – and before many minutes had gone, Jinks gave a startled shout.

'I say! What's happened! Look at our chair!'

The others looked – but it wasn't a chair any

longer! It was a big, fat baby in a frilly dress and a white bonnet!

The goblins set it down on the grass in astonishment and horror. A baby! What in the world were they to do with a baby? It was so big too – almost as big as they were!

'This is the sort of thing that always happens in Dreamland,' said Jinks, with a groan. 'Things change before you know where you are. What are we going to do?'

'Hoo-hoo-hoo!' wept the baby, very loudly.

'There, there!' said Tuppeny, patting it. 'I say, Jinks, it must be *somebody's* baby, you know. It isn't ours. We can't leave it here, so we'd better try and find out whose child it is.'

'Well, let Tuppeny stay with it whilst we go and find out,' said Feefo. 'We can ask at the big house whose garden we seem to be in. It may even belong there!'

'All right,' said Jinks. 'You can stay here with the baby, Tuppeny. We won't be long.'

Off they went and soon came to a big rambling house which seemed to have no doors at all, no matter where Jinks and Feefo looked.

'Dreamland is a silly place,' said Feefo, impatiently. 'Nothing's ever right.'

Suddenly, round the corner of the house came a fat nurse, wheeling a large pram. She was shaking it gently as she wheeled it and singing a little song. Jinks clutched Feefo and pointed.

'Let's ask her about the baby!'

So they went up to her and bowed.

'If you please, have you lost a baby?' asked Jinks, politely.

'Lost a baby!' said the nurse, in astonishment. She looked into her pram and then gave a loud howl.

'She's gone! The little darling's gone! Oh, where is she, where is she?'

'We know where she is,' said Jinks, eagerly. 'She's down the garden. Bring the pram and you can have her.'

'Did you take her? Oh, you wicked little goblins!' cried the nurse, angrily. 'You wait till I get my precious baby back and I'll soon show you what I'll do to you! Oh, the poor precious thing!'

The goblins ran back down the garden, the nurse following with the pram. But when they reached Tuppeny, they stopped in dismay. There was no baby with him – only a large grey donkey that brayed loudly. It had on the baby's white bonnet and looked very strange.

'Where's the baby?' they asked Tuppeny.

'I don't know,' said Tuppeny, in dismay. 'It suddenly seemed to change into this donkey. I couldn't stop it.'

'Well, *now* what shall we do?' cried Feefo, crossly. 'We've found a nurse who's lost a baby. Look, here she is, and she's jolly angry, too!'

They turned to see her – but even as they

looked the nurse was no longer a nurse but a
butcher boy with a large white apron tied round
him and the pram was a two-wheeled cart! The
donkey backed into the shafts of the cart, the
butcher whistled and off they went down the path
at a spanking trot, the donkey's bonnet flapping
up and down as it went.

'Well, thank goodness that's got rid of the
baby!' said Feefo.

'Yes, but we've lost our armchair,' said Tuppeny,
sorrowfully.

'Come on,' said Jinks. 'We've got to ask where
we can find the Blue Bird.'

They went down the path and out of the gate.
Before long they met a man riding on a fat pig and
they asked him if he knew where they could find
the Blue Bird.

'Yes, it lives with its master, Brownie Longbeard, in the last cottage in the next village,' said
the man, and rode off. The pig had changed into
a cat whilst he was speaking, but he didn't seem
to notice.

The three goblins soon came to the next village.
It was a perfectly round place, and each house was
set close to its neighbour in a tight circle. So there
was neither a last house nor a first one!

Jinks knocked at a door and a little girl opened
it.

'Please could you tell me which is the last house
in this village?' he asked.

'Yes, it's next to the last but one,' said the little girl, and slammed the door, which immediately disappeared.

'Well, *that's* a lot of help!' said Jinks, in disgust.

'I know!' said Tuppeny, beaming. 'If Feefo can make a sound like bird-seed, perhaps the Blue Bird will look out of one of the windows and we shall see which house the last one is!'

So Feefo made a very strange sound, which made half a hundred brown sparrows at once fly straight on to his head and shoulders! He shook them off, and the three looked carefully round the village. To their enormous surprise they saw a blue bird looking out of *every* window there!

'Oh, well, seeing there are so many blue birds, we might as well choose one,' said Feefo, and he went towards a house. But as he got near to it the blue bird disappeared and seemed to be nothing but a blue curtain waving in the wind. The next blue bird turned out to be a blue vase, and the next one was a piece of blue ribbon tying up a curtain. It was all very puzzling. Dreamland was certainly a peculiar place.

At last, just as they were in despair, they heard the sound of footsteps and saw a brownie coming up to them, with a beautiful blue bird sitting on his shoulder. He had a long grey beard that swept the ground and looked very old and wise.

'Hurrah!' said Jinks, in delight. 'Here's the Blue Bird. Hi, Brownie, would you do something for us?'

'It depends what it is,' said the brownie, stopping. The Blue Bird opened its beak and made a noise like a peacock. Tuppeny nearly jumped out of his skin, for it was a very loud, harsh noise.

'Well, we would very much like a feather out of your bird's tail,' said Feefo. The Blue Bird at once gave a yell and flew straight up into the air. It went to a chimney pot on one of the houses and swooped down it. 'Ho!' thought Tuppeny, 'so that's where it lives.' He looked at the name on the house. It was 'Here-I-Live'. Tuppeny thought that would be nice and easy to remember.

'I might get you a feather if you'll do something for *me*,' said the brownie. 'I want a parcel delivered to Mister Snooze on Up-and-Down Hill. If you take it there safely I'll see what I can do about a feather.'

'Oh, thank you!' said Jinks, delighted. The brownie ran into his house and came out with a large square parcel done up in brown paper and tied with string. He gave it to Jinks.

It was very heavy. Jinks staggered under the weight of it, but Feefo soon gave him a hand. They set off in the direction of Up-and-Down Hill, pointed out to them by Brownie Longbeard.

Halfway there Feefo said he must have a rest, so down they sat, putting the parcel on the ground. But no sooner was it there than it grew six legs and scuttled away from them! Tuppeny jumped up with a shout and caught it.

It grew two hands and gave him a hard smack on the nose! Feefo took it from poor Tuppeny and tucked it under his arm. Then it turned itself into a sort of treacly parcel and flowed away quickly.

'My gracious!' said Feefo, in despair, trying to get hold of it. 'Here, Jinks, you take it!'

Jinks took it and at once the paper fell off, the string became untied and hundreds of papers dropped out and began to fly about in the wind. It was dreadful.

'This is like a bad dream,' said Jinks. He and the others began to pick up the papers as fast as they could, for the wind flew off with them at once. Then, quite suddenly, before they knew how it happened, all the papers flew together, the parcel was done up and tied, and there it was, perfectly good and still, under Jinks's arm!

'Don't let's waste any more time!' said Jinks, and they set off at a run to Mister Snooze's house, which they could see quite clearly on the hill.

The parcel behaved itself till they got there. They knocked on the door but there was no answer. Only a strange noise could be heard. Feefo peeped in at the window and saw Mister Snooze sitting in a chair, fast asleep.

'Let's leave the parcel in at the window and go,' said Feefo. So they pushed the parcel in and turned to go. But that wretched parcel began to make a noise like a horse neighing and woke up Mister Snooze at once. He rushed to the window and called out, 'Hi, you! That's my horse got out of the field again. Put him back, will you?'

'No, it isn't!' said Jinks. 'It's the parcel we brought you from Brownie Longbeard making that noise!'

A loud neigh sounded in his ear and he turned round – and to his enormous astonishment he saw a little horse just by him! How strange!

'You might take him to Longbeard's!' called Mister Snooze. 'He wants to borrow him to go to market.'

Jinks caught hold of the halter round the horse's neck and led him off. The others came with him, glad that the wretched parcel was at last delivered. The horse lagged behind a little after a bit, and Jinks pulled him. 'Come on, there, come on!'

He turned to see why the horse was so long in coming – and bless us all, there wasn't a horse on the end of the rope at all! There was a large hippopotamus!

'Jumping beetles!' shrieked Tuppeny, and took to his heels at once.

Jinks stared at the hippo in dismay, but it seemed quite harmless, if a little slow. It came quietly lumbering on, blinking at Jinks out of its little eyes.

'I don't know what Longbeard will say if he sees us bringing him a hippo instead of a horse,' said Jinks. But Tuppeny and Feefo were too far ahead to hear him. They didn't like hippos quite so close!

However, Jinks needn't have worried – because by the time the hippo reached the village it wasn't a hippo any more, but a nice fat pig, wearing, for some strange reason, galoshes on its four feet.

'Where does the brownie live?' asked Jinks as they came into the village.

'He lives at "Here-I-Live",' said Tuppeny, pleased that he had noticed the name.

The first house they looked at was called 'Here-I-Live', so Jinks went up the path and knocked at the front door. A cross-looking woman opened it and asked them what they wanted.

'Will you tell Longbeard we have come back?' said Jinks. The woman made a face at him and answered crossly.

'What are you talking about? Brownie Longbeard doesn't live here! He lives in the last house.'

'Well, Tuppeny, you are *silly*!' said Jinks, annoyed, going back down the path. 'You might have noticed the name of Longbeard's house properly. He doesn't live there!'

They went to the next house – and dear me, *that* was called 'Here-I-Live' too! And so was the next one – and the next one – and all of them. It was too silly for words.

There was nothing for it but to knock at every house, and find out if Longbeard lived there. They went all round the village, and, of course, it was the very last house they knocked at that was the right one.

'Well, everyone said Longbeard lived in the last house, and they were right,' said Jinks, gloomily. 'This is the silliest place ever I knew!'

Longbeard asked them in at once. He gave them some chocolate cakes which tasted of ginger and some cocoa to drink which tasted of lemonade. The Blue Bird sat on his shoulder all the time and blinked at the goblins. In its tail was a very long feather indeed and Jinks longed to have it.

Longbeard didn't seem to mind at all having a pig instead of a horse, to ride to market, so that was all right. When they had finished eating Jinks reminded him politely that he had promised them a feather out of the Blue Bird's tail.

'Well, you can get one if you like,' said the brownie, grinning. Jinks was delighted. He at once made a grab at the Blue Bird who gave a loud squawk and flew round the room. The three goblins chased it, each trying to get the long blue feather. But that bird was very artful. It always just managed to get out of the way. It hid behind things, it flew up to the ceiling, it ran under the table.

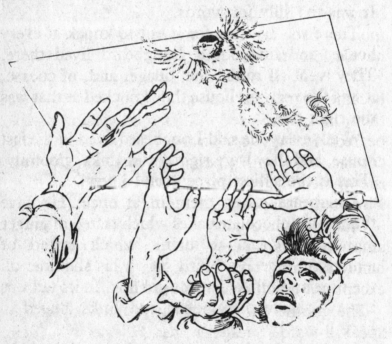

But at last Jinks caught it. Yes, he actually did! He got it by the tail and carefully pulled at the longest feather there so as not to hurt the lovely bird.

And even as he pulled, a peculiar and most annoying thing happened. The bird changed into a blue monkey and goodness, gracious me, Jinks pulled its tail out! There it was in his hands, a blue, hairy tail, not a bit feathery, not a bit like a bird's! The monkey darted up to the top of the curtains and sat there, tailless, scolding Jinks hard in a loud, chattering voice.

'Look here!' said Jinks, crossly, to the grinning brownie. 'This won't do, you know! Change that monkey back into a bird again at once and let me have a feather. You promised!'

The brownie only laughed loudly, and Jinks became angry. He rushed at Longbeard – and then, in a trice, everything broke up and disappeared! It was very strange. The walls of the cottage fell in with a bang, the roof flew off, and the whole village, with the brownie and the Blue Bird too, disappeared like a flash of lightning.

Only the three goblins were left. They stood amazed, Jinks holding the monkey's tail in his hand. Nothing was left of the village at all – except one small armchair just behind them.

The goblins sat down in it, too astonished to speak a word. Suddenly they felt sleepy. Their heads fell forward and Feefo began to snore gently.

And, as soon as they were asleep, that little armchair rose up into the air and grew wings! It flew away to Heyho Village, came gently to the ground, pushed open the door of Hollyhock Cottage and went inside.

After a short while the three goblins woke up. They looked all round and were most astonished to find that they were home again – and even more surprising still, in their own armchair! Wasn't that amazing?

'It must all have been a dream!' said Tuppeny, yawning.

'No, it wasn't,' said Jinks, flapping the monkey tail at him. 'Look here!'

Just then, there was a knock on the door and Fairy Tiptoe came in.

'I heard you talking, so I knew you were back,' she said, excitedly. 'Did you manage to get me that feather?'

'No,' said Jinks, sadly, shaking his head. He held out the monkey tail. 'This is all we got.'

'But that *is* just the very feather I want!' said Tiptoe, and she took it gladly from Jinks – and as she took it, it changed into a long, waving blue feather! It was very extraordinary.

'You darlings!' cried Tiptoe, and gave them each a kiss. They *were* pleased. 'Now you shall come to tea with me and taste my new chocolate cake. It's very good. And I will give you each ten pieces of gold for being so clever.

'We don't want the gold,' said Jinks. 'We just want your friendship, Tiptoe. We'd *love* to come to tea with you!'

A Peculiar Adventure in Dreamland

That new chocolate cake *was* lovely! Jinks had two pieces, Tiptoe had one, Feefo had three and Tuppeny had four – so there wasn't much left, as you can imagine!

The Castle of the Booming Giant

The very next day there came another customer to Hollyhock Cottage. This was a small red dwarf who drove up in a bright green motorcar, which stopped outside the cottage and hooted very loudly indeed.

Jinks and the others peeped out of the window. When they saw the red dwarf they didn't like the look of him at all. He was a most disagreeable creature, dressed very beautifully in red satin trimmed with real gold buttons. In his hat was a jewelled feather and on his long nose were spectacles set with diamonds that flashed brilliantly every time he moved his head.

He hooted loudly again.

'I suppose he wants us to rush out and bow to him,' said Jinks, in disgust. 'Well, he can want!'

'Hoot-hoot-hoot!' went the car, and all the neighbours put their heads out of their windows to see what the noise was about.

Jinks stuck his head out too.

'What are you hooting for?' he shouted. 'Is there something in your way?'

'I want to speak to you,' said the dwarf.

'Well, *I* don't want to speak to *you*!' said Jinks, and slammed the window.

'You'll be sorry!' shouted the dwarf, angrily. 'I'm the richest dwarf in the world, and I can pay you well for anything you sell me.'

'Well, let me sell you some good manners, then!' said Jinks, opening his window and grinning at the angry dwarf. 'They don't cost much and you could do with them!'

The dwarf glared at Jinks. Then he opened the door of his car, got out and marched up the path.

Tuppeny was frightened. 'Jumping beetles, Jinks, here he comes! You oughtn't to have spoken to him like that.'

The dwarf knocked at the door. Jinks opened it and the dwarf came in.

'You're a bold one, to talk to *me* like that!' he said to Jinks. 'No one has ever spoken to me like that before. You must be very brave.'

'Did you want to buy some good manners, then?' asked Jinks, smiling wickedly.

'No,' said the dwarf, shortly. 'Don't be rude any more. I don't like it. I should have gone away when you spoke to me so cheekily, but because I thought it was brave of you to say what you really thought, I hoped you might be the kind of fellow who could get me what I wanted.'

'And what is that?' asked Jinks, Tuppeny and Feefo, all together.

'I want to buy the pair of red shoes that the Booming Giant has,' said the red dwarf. 'I believe he will sell them if you offer him three of my largest diamonds to wear in his cap.'

'The Booming Giant!' said Jinks, astonished. 'But my goodness me, we'd never come back if we went to see *him*!'

'Oh, I'll give you a Get-away spell,' said the red dwarf. 'He will certainly want to keep you prisoners, but he won't be able to if you use the Get-away spell.'

'All right,' said Jinks. 'We'll get the red shoes for you – though why you want them I can't imagine, when you can buy any amount at the cobbler's!'

'Never you mind what I want them for,' said the red dwarf. He put his hand in his pocket and took out a small leather wallet. He undid it and the three goblins gasped – for inside lay three of the largest and most beautiful diamonds they had ever seen! They winked and blinked as if they were alive.

'Jumping beetles!' said Tuppeny, in awe.

Then the dwarf took out a little blue box and showed the goblins a tiny pinch of purple powder inside it.

'This is the Get-away spell,' he said. 'All you have to do when you want to escape from the

Booming Giant is to scatter this powder in front of you. Then you will get away perfectly easily.'

Jinks took the wallet of diamonds and the blue box and put them safely into his basket.

'We'll go tomorrow to the Booming Giant,' he promised. 'We'll let you know when we've got the red shoes for you.'

The dwarf said goodbye, ran down to his car and drove away. The three goblins rubbed their hands and did a little dance. 'We shall soon be very, very rich!' they sang. 'We shall soon be very, very rich!'

They went to say goodbye to Fairy Tiptoe next

door, and she was sorry to hear they were going away.

'It won't be for long,' said Tuppeny, hopefully.

'How do we go, Jinks?' asked Feefo, waggling his ears, feeling excited to think there was another adventure coming.

'The Booming Giant lives in the Thunder-Clouds,' said Jinks, who was busy unfolding a map. 'Look, there they are. We've got to go to the Sugar Mountain, whose tip sticks into the clouds. The Booming Giant lives in a castle at the top.'

Next morning they set off together, and went to catch the little train that ran through the country-side to the Sugar Mountain. They took their tickets from the big grey rabbit who sat in the ticket-office and waited for the train.

It came puffing in at last, not much bigger than a toy train, with open trucks to sit in, instead of proper carriages. It was full of gnomes and brownies, all chattering hard, and it was difficult to find places.

Nobody would move up and make room for the three goblins. But Feefo soon made them! He made a noise like a growling tiger, and you should have seen how those gnomes and brownies got out of his way! There was plenty of room at once!

Jinks and Tuppeny giggled. 'Where's the tiger?' called Jinks to Feefo. 'Is he going to run along beside our truck?'

Goodness, how those gnomes and brownies shivered and shook.

'That will teach them manners!' whispered Tuppeny to Jinks.

The train went on for a long way and all the gnomes and brownies got out at a station called 'Fair Station.' There was always a fair there, and the goblins could hear the roundabouts playing in the distance.

Tuppeny wanted to leave the train and go and look at the fair, but Jinks said no, certainly not! They were on business, and it would be silly to go to a fair with three large diamonds. Somebody would be sure to steal them.

So on they went in the little, puffing train. It went into a dark tunnel and then out again. It went over a long, high bridge that ran across a very wide green river on which floated tiny blue-sailed boats. It looked very pretty, and Tuppeny was so interested in leaning out and watching the ships that he very nearly tumbled right down into the river below.

Jinks caught him just in time. He grabbed him by the leg and pulled him into the truck.

'Ooh! Don't!' said Tuppeny, very red in the face, rubbing his leg. 'You clumsy thing, Jinks, hurting my leg like that!'

'Well, really!' said Jinks, crossly. 'I just saved your life, Tuppeny, and that's all the thanks I get! You might have been in the river by now.'

'Well, next time you save my life you needn't grab my leg quite so hard,' grumbled Tuppeny, sulkily.

The train went on and on, past Twisty Station and Tumble-down Station and many more. At last the three goblins gave a shout and pointed to a curious hill in the distance. It shone like white sugar, and reached up so high that its top was quite hidden in some very black, thundery-looking clouds.

'There's the Sugar Mountain!' cried Jinks. 'Hurrah! We're nearly there.'

The train puffed right up to the foot of the curious, sugary mountain and then stopped at a little station there called Sugar Station. The three goblins got out of their truck and the train went on round the mountain.

'The thing is – how do we get up?' said Feefo, rubbing his long nose.

'There aren't any steps,' said Tuppeny.

'The sugar slips dreadfully when you tread on it,' said Jinks. 'It's like loose white sand. We'll never be able to get up this hill!'

Just at that moment a most surprising thing came round the corner of the hill. It was a camel! There was no one with it, which made it all the more astonishing. It came straight up to the three goblins and knelt down in front of them.

'What does it want?' said Tuppeny, getting behind the others in a fright.

238

'It's come to take us up the Sugar Mountain!' cried Jinks, delighted. 'Camels can walk easily on sand, so this one won't find it at all difficult to climb up on sugar! Good camel! Fine camel!'

The camel made rather a nasty, cross sort of snort that Tuppeny didn't like at all. Jinks hastily got on its hump and Feefo and Tuppeny climbed on to its neck. The camel stood up and began to climb the Sugar Mountain. The goblins had to hold on very tightly, for the camel slanted steeply as it climbed and it swayed from side to side in a very alarming manner.

'Get up, there! Get up, there!' cried Jinks, encouragingly, but the camel only made a few more nasty noises. It really was a very bad-tempered sort of beast.

The mountain was very high. There seemed to be no paths of any sort, no grass, no trees, no bushes – only just gleaming white sugar. The camel went up and up, grunting and gurgling, and the goblins clung on for dear life.

'We're coming to the Thunder-Clouds!' cried Jinks, at last. The others looked up. Sure enough, not very far above them were the heavy-looking purple clouds they had seen from the train.

'I can see the giant's castle in the clouds!' said Tuppeny, nearly falling off the camel as he looked upwards. 'Ooh! Jumping beetles, it *is* a monster castle!'

So it was! It was bigger than anything the goblins had ever imagined, and its towers and turrets rose gleaming towards the sun, which peeped here and there between the moving clouds.

'Gurgle-grr-gurgle,' said the camel, in its cross voice and knelt down on a cloud, which, although it seemed very flimsy indeed to look at, seemed to be hard enough to walk on, though it felt rather spongy to the foot.

'It's like walking on a terribly thick carpet,' said Tuppeny. 'I do hope I shan't suddenly walk in a hole and fall right down to the earth below.'

'You'd better take my hand in case you do,' said Feefo. 'You're a dreadful goblin for falling out of things.'

Hand in hand they walked over the soft thunderclouds towards the towering castle. A long flight of steps led up to a gleaming black door, set with yellow stones of some kind.

'What are we going to do?' whispered Tuppeny to Jinks. 'Are you just going straight in to ask for the shoes, or what?'

'Yes, I think so,' said Jinks, boldly. 'I've got those three lovely diamonds to offer the giant. I expect he'll be pleased to give us the shoes in exchange.'

So they knocked at the great door, and it opened slowly before them. A booming voice, like the wind at sea, came through the door.

'BRING THE WASHING IN, AND PUT IT DOWN, MRS DOWELL.'

Jinks and the other two stepped inside the door, and blinked in amazement, for there, before them, was the very biggest giant they had ever seen in their lives. He was as tall as the tallest tree, and his eyes were as large as cartwheels and so blue that they seemed like ponds in his face.

'If you please, we're not the washing,' said Jinks.

'SPEAK MORE LOUDLY,' said the giant, not looking up from the book he was reading.

'WE'RE NOT THE WASHING!' shouted Jinks, Tuppeny and Feefo, together. That made the giant look up and he seemed most surprised to see the three goblins.

'Then what are you?' he boomed.

'We're three goblins who have come to buy something from you,' said Jinks, boldly. 'We want a pair of red shoes you have, and we have brought three large diamonds to pay for them.'

'Let me see them,' said the giant, greedily. Jinks undid the wallet and the three stones glittered brilliantly before the astonished giant.

The giant calmly put down his enormous hand and took the wallet from Jinks.

'Thank you!' he said, with a thunderous laugh. 'I'll keep them. As for the shoes, they are not for sale.'

'But you can't keep the diamonds if you don't give us the shoes!' cried Jinks, horrified.

'Can't I?' grinned the giant, showing two rows of white teeth as large as piano keys. 'I can! And what's more, I'm going to keep you too! Ho, ho, that's a good joke!'

Tuppeny began to weep. He was scared out of his life. Feefo went red with rage and Jinks for once in a way really didn't know *what* to do or say!

The giant picked them all up and popped them into a big wastepaper basket, so high and tall that the goblins couldn't possibly get out of it.

'You stay there for a bit,' he said. 'I'll sell you to the Wandering Wizard when he comes to see me tonight. He'll be glad to have you.'

The three goblins crouched together in the bottom of the basket.

'It's all your fault for being so silly as to walk in boldly like that,' wept Tuppeny to Jinks. 'We ought to have found out what sort of a giant he was first.'

'I'm awfully hungry,' said Feefo, sighing. 'I wish we had something to eat.'

Jinks opened his basket. He really did feel ashamed of himself to think he had landed his friends into such terrible trouble. To Feefo's great delight there were packets of chocolate and three apples in the basket. The mouse was there too, just beginning to nibble one of the apples. Jinks took that one for himself, smacked the mouse and divided up the rest of the food between the others. They all ate in silence, wondering whatever they could do to escape.

They tried to get out of the basket. It was no good at all, and the giant heard them scrabbling about and roared to them to keep quiet.

'I'm trying to work out a spell!' he boomed. 'How can I work when you make such a noise, like a lot of fidgety mice. Be quiet or I'll put you in the dustbin.'

After that the goblins didn't dare to move! The afternoon came and the giant got himself tea. Darkness fell and the giant lit a great lamp that shone almost as brightly as the sun itself! He bent over his spell, frowning.

Suddenly Feefo, who had been thinking very hard, made a noise like six cats fighting each

243

other. It made Jinks and Tuppeny almost jump out of their lives, and they glared angrily at Feefo, who calmly went on making the extraordinary noise.

'Drat those cats!' shouted the giant, crossly. He went to the window, threw it open and shouted 'BE QUIET, WILL YOU?' to the cats he thought were quarrelling outside his window. For a while Feefo made no noise – then he began again, and this time it seemed as if there must be fifty cats, by the hissing and snarling, wailing and groaning!

The giant jumped up in a rage and took a big jug of water to the window. He threw the water where he thought the cats were and Feefo stopped snarling at once. The giant went back to his work.

Then once more Feefo began, this time like a hundred cats, and the giant went nearly mad with rage. He threw his boots at the cats, he threw a kettle and he threw a chair. Then he flung open his china cupboard and was going to throw out all his cups and saucers when Feefo poked his head nearly out of the basket, standing on Jinks's shoulders.

'Please, sir, I can stop those cats for you, and send them away.'

'You!' said the giant, scornfully. 'Why, they are giant cats and would gobble you up like a mouse, goblin.'

'Well, let me try,' said Feefo.

'Very well,' said the giant, grinning, 'but don't blame me if you get eaten, that's all! And mind you come back once you've scared them away!'

'Oh, yes!' said Feefo. He whispered something very quickly in Jinks's ear and then the giant hauled him out of the basket.

'Before I go, do tell me where you keep the red shoes,' begged Feefo. 'I know it's no good asking you for them, but I *would* like to know where they are kept.'

245

'Well, much good may it do you!' said the giant. 'I keep them in my pocket!'

Feefo said nothing more, but went to the door, which the giant opened for him, and slipped out into the darkness. He began to shout as if he were scolding a great many cats, and very soon there came a sound as if dozens of cats were scampering away. The giant was pleased. He went to the door and looked out for Feefo – but he was nowhere to be seen.

'Come back!' shouted the giant. But Feefo didn't come back. He was safely at the bottom of the Sugar Mountain, having rolled all the way down in a great hurry!

'Let me go and find him!' cried Tuppeny to the giant. 'Give me a lantern and let me go. Feefo can't see in the dark and maybe he has lost his way going after the cats. I will bring him safely back.'

The giant lighted a small lantern and gave it to Tuppeny. It was almost as big as he was, but he managed to carry it. He ran out of the door, calling Feefo. But as soon as he was out, he threw the lantern down and rolled himself over and over in the sugar, right down to the very bottom of the hill, just as Feefo had done.

He bumped into Feefo, who caught him and hugged him. 'What about Jinks?' asked Tuppeny.

'Oh, he's going to get the red shoes when the giant is asleep, and then use the Get-away spell,' said Feefo, grinning in the darkness. 'We'll wait here for him!'

'I do hope he won't be long!' sighed Tuppeny, who was very tired of this adventure. 'I want to be safely at home in dear little Hollyhock Cottage!'

Jinks and the
Surprising Shoes

Jinks sat at the bottom of the wastepaper basket alone, glad that Tuppeny and Feefo had managed to escape. The giant was very angry when he found that the others did not come back. He roared and stamped till the castle rocked quite dangerously on the clouds.

Then he looked into the basket and shook his fist at Jinks, who pretended to be frightened. He wasn't really, because he had the Get-away spell safely in his basket, and knew he could escape at any time – but he meant to get those magic red shoes first!

'I'm going to have a nap until my friend, the Wandering Wizard, comes,' roared the giant. 'And don't you think you can play any tricks on me as your friends have done, because you can't!'

'Oh, no, I shouldn't dream of it,' answered Jinks, politely. The giant went to a big armchair and lay back on the cushions. He closed his eyes and in a moment or two there came the sound of snoring. It sounded like fifty motorcars starting up their engines, and almost deafened Jinks.

He grinned to himself, and then opened his basket. The little white mouse was there, and when Jinks spoke to it, it pricked up its tiny ears and listened hard.

'I want you to nibble a hole in this big wastepaper basket I'm in,' said Jinks. 'Can you do that, little Whiskers?'

The mouse squeaked and jumped out of Jinks's tray at once. It ran to the side of the big waste-paper basket and began to nibble hard. Soon there was quite a big hole in it, and Jinks was able to make it bigger by tearing it open with his hands. The mouse went on nibbling and nibbling. It had very sharp teeth and was pleased to be able to help Jinks.

'Get back on to the tray,' whispered Jinks to the mouse, when he saw that he could just squeeze through the hole. The mouse ran up Jinks's leg and hopped on to the tray. Jinks shut it up and made it into a basket again. Then, taking a peep through the hole first, he squeezed through and found himself standing on the floor of the giant's hall.

The giant was still snoring loudly, and the castle shook to the sound. Jinks stole quietly up to the sleeping giant and climbed silently up the chair-leg. He squeezed himself on to a small piece of the armchair seat and tried to see into the giant's pockets. They were as big as caves to Jinks!

He could see nothing inside at all. It was too dark. So there was nothing for it but to creep right into the pocket and see if the red shoes were there!

Jinks was brave. He began to worm himself into the pocket, hoping and hoping that it was the right one. It was! He felt a pair of shoes there, not very big, almost his size. He carefully pulled at them and took them into his hands. Then he began to crawl out of the giant's pocket.

And just at that very moment there came a thundering knock at the castle door which woke up the giant!

It was the Wandering Wizard! He came stalking in, crying, 'Good evening, good evening! And how is my friend the Booming Giant tonight?'

The giant jumped up and shook hands. The Wandering Wizard was a strange fellow with a long beard that he kept tied in a neat knot at his waist. He seemed quite a jolly chap, and Jinks, peeping out of the giant's pocket, wondered if he were very powerful. It would be dreadful if he was powerful enough to stop the Get-away spell from working!

'I've got a surprise for you!' said the Booming Giant to the wizard. 'I had three little green goblins here today, and I thought I'd give them to you for servants. But two got away, and I've only one left.'

'Dear dear, stars and moon, couldn't you manage to keep the lot of them?' said the wizard. 'You are really rather a stupid fellow, Booming, though I like you well enough. Well, where's the third goblin?'

'In that wastepaper basket,' said Booming.

The wizard went over to it.

'There's nothing there but a large hole in the side,' he said, surprised. 'Are you playing a joke on me?'

'Of course not!' said the giant, astonished. He looked into the basket too, and when he saw that Jinks had escaped he went as red as a tomato with rage.

'So he's gone too,' he roared. 'Well, I've got their diamonds, anway. Look, Wizard – three beauties to put into my cap. They came to get my magic red shoes. Aha, little do they know the magic that is in those shoes. Only those who wear the shoes know that!'

'Where are the shoes?' asked the wizard. The giant put his hand into his pocket – and brought out Jinks! Jinks had carefully packed the shoes into his basket for safety and had also quickly taken out the Get-away spell which was in its little box.

'Why, here's the third goblin!' cried the giant. 'In my pocket! After those shoes, I'll be bound! Oh, the rascal, oh, the wretch, he's taken them, he's taken them!'

Jinks slid out of the giant's hand and jumped to

the ground. He ran about the kitchen, laughing, for he thought he would tease the giant.

'Ho ho ho!' he grinned. 'I've got the shoes, dear giant! Catch me if you can! Ho ho!'

Then began such a chase! The wizard ran after Jinks, and so did the lumbering giant! Jinks darted under sofas and tables, he ran into corners, he hid under rugs. The wizard and the giant were quite out of breath trying to catch the slippery little goblin.

And at last the giant *did* catch him! He made a dart at him and his fingers closed over the

wriggling goblin – but at that very moment Jinks blew the purple powder out of the box and cried, 'Get me away spell!' – and hey presto a big wind came, swept him out of the giant's hand, through the open window and down to the bottom of the Sugar Mountain!

Tuppeny and Feefo had fallen fast asleep there, waiting for him. They woke with a jump as he rolled into them, and when they struck a match and found it really was Jinks, they were too delighted for words.

Jinks told them all that had happened and showed them the red shoes safely packed in his basket. The white mouse was curled up in one of them and looked very comfortable indeed. Jinks stroked him and called him a little hero for helping him to escape from the wastepaper basket.

'Let's make a cosy hole in this sugar and go to sleep again,' said Tuppeny, who was yawning widely. So they dug a big hole with their hands, crept into it, curled up together like kittens and fell sound asleep.

They awoke when the sun was high in the sky. The camel woke them by grunting and bubbling in their ear. He butted them with his nose and then knelt down to take them on his back.

Tuppeny was just about to get on him, when Jinks pulled him back.

'Don't be so silly!' he said. 'That camel would

only take you back to the castle! He won't take us home.'

'Oh, won't he?' said Tuppeny, who was often rather stupid. 'Well, I won't ride him then. Shoo, camel, shoo!'

But the camel wouldn't shoo. It made some very nasty noises and showed them its teeth – so the goblins decided they had better move away.

'We'll catch the first train back to our village,' said Jinks, firmly. 'Oh, do go away, camel. We don't WANT you!'

They soon left the camel behind and made their way to Sugar Station. The train came in and they got in. It was quite empty this time, so they had it to themselves. They passed all the stations they had passed before, and at last came to Fair Station. There was the fair beginning again! They could hear the music of the roundabouts and see the swings going high in the air.

'Oh, Jinks, dear Jinks, do let's go to the fair!' begged Tuppeny. 'We've done our work and got the red shoes, and it would be nice to have some play now. Besides, I'm very hungry and we could get breakfast at the fair. I know they have fried sausages and new bread because I can smell them from here.'

'Come on, then!' said Jinks. They all tumbled out of the train and were soon eating plates of steaming sausages and munching rolls of new bread. They drank hot coffee and felt very much better. Then they went on the roundabouts and on the swings and had a fine time.

Soon Jinks got excited and thought he would show off a bit. So he put his hat on his feet, turned himself upside down, and began to walk on his hands, just as he had done when Feefo and Tuppeny had first seen him.

But the fair-ground was muddy and Jinks's hands got very dirty. He remembered the red shoes in his basket and took them out. He slipped them on his hands and then began to walk upside down again, waggling his feet about with his hat on them, and dancing the red shoes about on his hands. Tuppeny and Feefo stood and giggled at him and the fair-folk shouted in delight.

Then, as Feefo and Tuppeny stood watching him Jinks began to walk out of the fair-ground! He walked right out of the gate!

'Hi, Jinks, where are you going?' shouted Tuppeny. 'Come back! You're going the wrong way!'

Jinks shouted something back but the others couldn't hear him. They ran after him and caught him up. Jinks was now walking on his hands very fast indeed and they could hardly keep up with him.

'Jinks, Jinks, where are you going, you silly?' cried Feefo, in fright.

'I can't stop!' cried Jinks, in a scared voice. 'It's

these magic shoes I've put on my hands, Feefo. They are taking me away. Can you get them off?'

Feefo tried his best to snatch at the shoes, but they went faster and faster as he tried to grab at them.

'Where are they taking you to?' shouted Tuppeny.

'Back to the Booming Giant's, I'm afraid,' yelled Jinks. 'I ought to have remembered that they are magic.'

At that the red shoes began to run so fast that Tuppeny and Feefo were left far, far behind. Soon poor Jinks was nothing but a small speck in the distance, hurrying back to the Sugar Mountain.

Tuppeny burst into tears.

'Now what are we to do?' he wailed. 'After getting the magic shoes and all, and escaping so nicely, there's poor Jinks gone back to the giant, who is sure to be very, *very* angry with him!'

Feefo was very pale. This was dreadful. Jinks had no Get-away spell this time.

'We'd better go back home,' he said, 'and see if the dwarf will give us another Get-away spell.'

So they jumped into the first train home and sent a message to the Red Dwarf. But when he heard what had happened, he laughed mockingly and shook his head.

'No,' he said. 'Get-away spells are most expensive. I'm not wasting any more on you. Let Jinks escape by himself this time. He shouldn't have been so stupid as to wear the red shoes. He knew they were magic. They always take anyone back to Sugar Mountain Castle.'

The two goblins were very unhappy. They sat in their big armchair together and even Feefo couldn't help the tears dripping down his cheeks.

There came a knock at the door, and Fairy Tiptoe came in. She was most astonished to see them so upset.

'Whatever's the matter?' she asked. 'And where's dear Jinks?'

They told her – and she listened with wide eyes.

'How dreadful!' she said. 'However can we rescue him?'

'We can't,' sobbed Tuppeny. 'Nobody can.'

'Oh, there must be a way,' said Tiptoe, thinking hard. 'I wonder if my grandmother would lend me her big, invisible cloak. Whoever wears it cannot be seen, you know. If we went to Sugar Mountain we might be able to smuggle Jinks away under the cloak.'

'Oh, let's try!' said Feefo, at once. So Tiptoe ran off to her grandmother's cottage and, as she had been very good and kind to the old lady, she was quite willing to lend her the magic cloak, if she promised not to tear it.

'Here it is!' said Tiptoe, coming in at the door. 'Now watch!'

She wrapped the shining blue cloak around her and at once she and the cloak disappeared entirely. It was marvellous! Both the goblins had to try it, of course, and laughed to see each other disappear like smoke!

They ate a good dinner and set off in the afternoon to go back to the Sugar Mountain, making plans on the way. The disagreeable camel was there, and they all clambered on to his back, though Tiptoe was just a bit afraid of him.

When they got to the Thunder-Clouds Tiptoe scooped some of the clouds out and made a little hiding-place for them so that the giant should not see them if he looked out of the window.

'Now this is my plan,' she said. 'First I will put on my magic cloak so that the giant won't see me, and I'll go and tell Jinks we're here and what to do. Then I'll come back to you and we'll see what to do next.'

The little fairy pulled the blue cloak round her and at once disappeared. She flew to the castle and entered in at the open window. Jinks was inside, tied to a table leg with a thick rope so that he couldn't move. The giant was peeling potatoes and talking loudly and scornfully to Jinks.

'Jinks, Jinks!' whispered Tiptoe, flying down beside him. He was startled because he could see nobody. He looked round, half scared.

'It's I, Tiptoe,' whispered the fairy, and she told

him how she and the others had come to rescue him.

'Can you think of a good plan?' she whispered. Jinks thought hard – and then he whispered into Tiptoe's ear. She nodded her head, gave him a little kiss on his right ear and flew out of the window again, pulling the giant's hair on the way, which astonished him very much indeed, for, of course, he could see nobody at all!

Tiptoe told Feefo and Tuppeny the plan and they agreed. They hid in the little cloud-hole until it was dark and then they crept out. Tuppeny and Feefo stood just outside the open window, and then, at a sign from Tiptoe, they began to make a noise!

Feefo made a noise like a roaring dragon in a temper! You should have heard him! It was perfectly marvellous, really! Even Tuppeny felt a bit frightened, though he knew it was only Feefo.

Tuppeny's part was easy. He had to shout at the top of his very big voice, crying, 'Come here, Dragon! Come here, I say!'

You see, they were pretending that a dragon had escaped and had come to the castle, and that Tuppeny was trying to catch him! Then Tiptoe did her part. She left the magic cloak with Feefo, who had it ready for Jinks when he should come out. She flew in at the window and blinked in the light of the bright lamp inside.

The giant had jumped to his feet in fright when he had heard the roaring of what he thought was a fierce dragon. Jinks was pretending to be frightened too, but he wasn't really, for he knew it was only Feefo.

'Oh, please, oh, please!' panted Tiptoe to the giant, pretending to be very much frightened. 'Will you come out and catch the dragon? He's escaped and we can't get him.'

'Of course I won't come and catch the dragon!' said the giant, hastily. 'I don't do silly things like that. Chase it down the mountain at once.'

'But he wants to come and see you,' said Tiptoe.

'See ME!' said the giant, in a terrible fright. 'Whatever for?'

'He says he's never tasted giant,' said Tiptoe.

'Ow-oo-ah!' yelled the giant, wondering wherever he could hide. But he was so big that he couldn't possibly hide himself anywhere.

'Has he ever tasted goblin?' suddenly asked the giant, hopefully.

'No, never,' said Tiptoe.

'Well, ask him if he'd like to taste a nice little goblin I've got here,' said the giant.

So Tiptoe called this out of the window and the dragon roared pleasantly that he would like very much to see the goblin. So the giant undid the rope that tied Jinks to the table and he ran out of the door. As soon as he reached Feefo that goblin threw the magic cloak around him, and around

260

himself and Tuppeny too, and stopped roaring. Tiptoe flew out and joined them. She crept under the big cloak, and they all lay still to see what would happen.

The giant was puzzled. Where was everyone? What had happened to the dragon? Where was that little fairy? And suddenly he saw that he had been tricked! It was no dragon! It was only somebody roaring like one!

With a roar even louder than Feefo's the angry giant rushed out of his castle with a bright

261

lantern. But no matter where he looked he could *not* see the goblins and the fairy. They were invisible, hidden under the magic cloak.

The giant ran shouting down the hill, trying to find them – and immediately Jinks ran back into the castle, opened a cupboard and took out the red shoes, which the giant had put there when he had taken them away from Jinks.

He popped them into his basket and ran to join the others.

'We'd better go down the other side of the Sugar Mountain,' said Tiptoe. 'Then we shan't run into the giant!'

It was much easier to climb down the other side. They were soon at the bottom. Then they saw the two red lights of the little train that ran around the mountain and they stopped it by pulling up the signal. They climbed on board and off they went, all very tired, very happy and very hungry.

They got home just as the sun was rising in the east. They were so sleepy that they could hardly eat the eggs that Tiptoe boiled for them or drink the cocoa she made.

'Oh, Tiptoe, we're *so* grateful to you!' said Jinks, half asleep. 'We'll never forget your help! Whatever the dwarf gives us for getting the red shoes, you shall share!'

And what do you think he gave them? Why, his green motorcar! So Tiptoe had to share that, and went for many a ride with the three goblins. Feefo usually drove because he was the most careful of the three, and when the horn went wrong, he could make a lovely honking noise. It was really lovely to hear him!

THE SECOND GREEN GOBLIN BOOK

The Strange Land of Topsy-Turvy

One morning, when Tuppeny, Feefo and Jinks, the three Goblins who ran a shop offering to get *anything* for *anyone*, were scrubbing their floor, they heard a great sound of cheering and hurrahing outside. They dropped their brushes and dusters to see what it was and rushed outside.

'Jumping beetles! It's the King and Queen of Fairyland!' cried Tuppeny, in excitement. 'Ooh! They're driving through Heyho Village! Let's go and cheer them!'

Just as they got to their gate the shining golden carriage of the King and Queen drove up. The goblins, thinking that the carriage was going past, waved their hands and cheered loudly. Tuppeny's voice was so enormous that it almost deafened everyone.

And then – and then – to the three goblins' great astonishment, the golden carriage

stopped at their very gate, and the King and Queen got out!

The goblins stood and stared with wide eyes and open mouths. Were their Majesties coming to visit *them*? Oh, no, surely not!

But, you know, they were! Yes, they walked right up to the gate, smiling, their jewelled crowns winking and blinking in the sun, and their long and beautiful wings gleaming like the wings of summer dragon-flies!

268

'Is this the shop belonging to Tuppeny, Feefo and Jinks?' asked the King.

'Yes – yes, certainly it is! Oh, yes, Your Majesty!' stammered Jinks, so much surprised that he didn't even move away from the gate.

Feefo, always the polite one, pulled him away and hissed into his ear. 'Can't you bow, you great stupid? Can't you even move out of the way?'

Jinks at once bowed deeply and made way for their Majesties. The King and Queen walked up the garden and into the little shop. Feefo got chairs, dusted them and put a pail of dirty water out of the way. Tuppeny was so overcome with awe and surprise that he didn't do or say anything at all. He just stood and stared.

'This is a great honour,' said Feefo to the King and Queen. 'Is there anything we can do for Your Majesties?'

'We have heard of you and the wonderful things you have done,' said the Queen, in a high, silvery voice like a swallow's. 'And as we are in a difficulty ourselves, we wondered if perhaps you could help us, as you have helped others.'

'Oh, Your Majesty, we'd love to!' said Jinks, standing first on one leg and then on the other, in the greatest delight. He could hardly keep from stroking the Queen's fine silky hair, that shone like golden sunlight. What a day this was! What an honour!

'This is our difficulty,' said the King. 'In Topsy-Turvy Land there lives an Enchanter, called Know-All, and he's just like his name. In fact, he knows too much, and his magic and enchantments are getting far too powerful for our happiness. He can spirit away fairies and elves, and we don't know where they've gone to. So we wondered if you could go to Topsy-Turvy Land and capture him for us.'

'Jumping beetles!' said Tuppeny, in the greatest alarm. He didn't at all like the idea of capturing a powerful enchanter. Feefo looked a little startled, but Jinks, as usual, was only too pleased to have a job to do. He beamed all over his jolly face at once.

'Yes, Your Majesty, we'll see to that at once for you. You can trust us! We'll do our very best.'

'For reward we will give you a palace on a hill, with a most marvellous view,' said the Queen. The goblins looked at one another. A palace! My, wouldn't they be grand! They would be like princes!

'Well, that's settled then,' said the King,

rising. 'Thank you very much. Let us know when you have captured the Enchanter and we will deal with him.'

Their Majesties went back to their golden carriage, waved goodbye and drove off, their eight white horses galloping fast down the village street. As soon as they were gone, their friend, the fairy Tiptoe, came rushing in to hear what the visit had been about.

But when she heard what they had to do, she grew pale and shook her head.

'You'll never capture Know-All,' she said.

271

'He is one of the most powerful and wicked enchanters in the whole world. He is worse than a bad witch. You are clever, Jinks darling, but not so clever as Know-All.'

'D-d-d-d-don't let's g-g-g-go!' stammered Tuppeny, in a fright.

But Jinks only grinned. He had a great belief in himself, and besides, hadn't he promised the King and Queen to try? He couldn't break his word.

They took out their maps and looked up Topsy-Turvy Land. It was rather a long way away. First they had to go through Pixie-Land, then over the Land of Night and last of all through the Grumbling Wood. Ooh dear!

Tuppeny didn't like the sound of things at all.

'Well, Tuppeny, you can stay at home, if you like, and mind the shop,' said Jinks. But Tuppeny wouldn't hear of that. Yes, he was afraid, but he wasn't a coward. He was coming too!

'I'll mind the shop for you,' said Tiptoe. 'But, oh, I do hope you won't be too long, goblins, because I shall be dreadfully worried about you.'

The next day they set off for Pixie-Land. They drove away in their little green motor-car

272

and Tiptoe waved to them from the gate. By the afternoon they had come to Pixie-Land. It was a pretty place, full of houses built of big toadstools, painted all kinds of bright colours. The pixies were little chattering folk, and the goblins waved cheerfully to them as they went by.

They had tea in Pixie-Land at a Toadstool tea-house, and a very good tea it was, especially some little pink cakes made of ripe wild strawberries and moonlight sugar. Tuppeny ate so many that he fell asleep in the car afterwards and didn't wake up until they were in the Land of Night. This was a strange land, always dark, even in the daytime, with great silver stars in the sky and a moon that looked three times as big as it ought to be. Only night-time creatures lived there – big, silent-winged owls that hooted frighteningly in Jinks's ear, black bats that squeaked piercingly as they flew over the car, and strange, shadowy creatures that fled out of the way of the headlights.

'I only hope our car doesn't break down here,' said Jinks, a little bit scared.

'Jumping beetles!' said Tuppeny, in a fright. 'Do you think it will?'

But it didn't. It chugged on well and at last

273

the sun rose on the Grumbling Wood, which stood next to the Land of Night.

The Grumbling Wood was a very difficult place to drive in. Big tree-roots suddenly stood up in the car's way and bushes seemed to appear out of nothing. The trees were tall and dark, and their leaves were queer. They were silver on the upper surface and black underneath, and when the wind blew the whole forest shimmered and shone in the strangest way.

And it grumbled! The trees groaned and grunted. The bushes sighed as if their hearts were breaking. Even the flowers hung their heads down and made a curious whining noise that could just be heard. It was a most unhappy place.

'These wretched tree-roots that keep popping up and nearly upsetting us!' grumbled Feefo – but Jinks nudged him sharply on the arm and spoke to him in a low whisper.

'Now, Feefo, don't grumble, whatever you do! Those who grumble belong to the wood and we don't want to stay here for the rest of our lives! You just watch, and you'll see some folk who have grumbled and groaned when they went through here and have had to stay for always!'

Feefo and Tuppeny looked out – and sure enough, here and there in the wood were some odd, unhappy-looking folk, with long faces. Some were scolding each other. Some were walking along, grumbling to themselves. Some were sighing at the heavy bundles they carried.

'My goodness, I shan't say a single grumble again!' said Feefo, startled. 'I shouldn't like to live with these grumblers in this strange, Grumbling Wood!'

At last, almost jolted to bits by the jutting tree-roots, the unexpected bushes and the low-hanging branches, the goblins left the

275

Grumbling Wood behind, and came to Topsy-Turvy Land. And here they really had to stop the car and gaze in astonishment.

For everything was topsy-turvy! Even the houses were built upside down. The people walked on their hands as Jinks sometimes did, and wore hats on their feet. The dogs had cats' tails, and the cats barked like dogs. Horses wore horns and the cows had coats like sheep. Really, the goblins could hardly believe their eyes!

Then they saw a large notice standing by the roadside. The notice was upside down, of course, but Jinks, by standing on his hands,

276

could easily read it. He came back to the others in excitement.

'I say, it's a notice from Know-All, the Enchanter. He says he is willing to give anyone a magic wand if they can do three things.'

'What are they?' asked Tuppeny and Feefo.

'One is – to show him something that nobody has ever seen before,' said Jinks. 'The second is to dance on the rock outside his palace and kick dust from it – and the third is to tell him what he is thinking!'

'Quite impossible, all three of them!' groaned Feefo. 'What's the use of bothering about a notice like that, Jinks?'

'What's the use!' cried Jinks. 'I'll tell you, Feefo! I can do all those things!'

Tuppeny and Feefo stared at him as if he had gone mad.

'Do you feel all right?' asked Tuppeny, anxiously. 'You're sure you don't feel ill, Jinks?'

'Don't be silly,' said Jinks, his bright eyes shining. 'My wits are as sharp as the Enchanter's, though I don't know nearly as much magic as he does! I tell you, I can do all these things!'

'You're a clever fellow, Jinks,' said Feefo. 'Well, tell us what you're going to do.'

But Jinks wouldn't. He said it was to be a

secret. He loved secrets and he loved surprising people. He jumped into the car again with the others and drove off through Topsy-Turvy Land. He stopped when he met a postman, walking on his hands, of course, and asked him where the sweep lived.

'That's his house over there,' said the postman, pointing. Jinks drove over to it and was surprised to find a little notice there that said –

> MISTER BISCUIT, THE SWEEP.
> ALL WASHING
> DONE HERE.

Mister Biscuit stood at his door, upside-down. 'Are you the sweep?' asked Jinks.

'Yes,' said Mister Biscuit.

'Have you any soot for sale?' said Jinks.

'Bless us, no!' said Mister Biscuit. 'I may be the sweep, but I don't sweep chimneys. I wash clothes.'

'What a funny idea!' said Feefo. 'I should hate to live in this land where everybody does the work that somebody else should do!'

'Who sweeps the chimneys, then?' asked Jinks, impatiently.

'Mister Chop, the washerman,' said Mister

Biscuit, getting out his handkerchief and blowing his ear with it. Tuppeny giggled and Mister Biscuit frowned at him.

'Where does he live?' asked Jinks.

'He lives at the fishmonger's,' said Mister Biscuit, and went indoors, angry with Tuppeny because he wouldn't stop laughing.

So Jinks drove to the fishmonger's, but as he sold cakes and bread, it was a very curious fish-shop. Mister Chop was a very black-looking man, so Jinks hoped he really was the sweep, though he kept a fish-shop that sold bread and cakes.

'Have you any soot for sale?' he asked the sweep.

'No, but I have plenty of bread,' said the sweep. 'If you want any soot, go and take it. There's some in a sack round the corner.'

Jinks told Tuppeny to get out and look. Soon Tuppeny came back with a small bag of very black soot.

'Put it in the back of the car under the seat,' said Jinks. So it was stowed away there.

Then Jinks drove straight towards a glittering palace that stood on a small hill in the distance. It was the right way up, which was curious to see in Topsy-Turvy Land. Jinks stopped the car behind a little group of big

trees and jumped out. He opened his basket
and made it into a tray. The little mouse was
there as usual, sitting up and washing its whiskers. By it was a nice, new-laid brown egg.

'Just what I was looking for!' said Jinks, in
delight. He took it out and put it into his
pocket, very carefully. Then he shook a green
cloak out of a brown parcel on the tray and a
green hat to match.

'What are all those things for?' said Tuppeny, in surprise.

'You'll see!' grinned Jinks. He put on the
green cloak, which had black cats embroidered
all over it, and set the hat on his cheeky head.
Then he took off his shoes and, to the other
goblins' great surprise, emptied a great deal of
soot into them. He gave them to Tuppeny to
hold and told him to take great care of them
and not drop them.

He put on a pair of slippers which he took
from his tray. Then he swept his cloak around
him and bowed grandly to Tuppeny and Feefo.

'Here you see before you, Minky-Monk, the
Mighty Magician and his two goblin servants,
come to pay a visit to his high-and-mightiness,
the Topsy-Turvy Enchanter!' he chanted.

Tuppeny and Feefo stared at him as if he

really were quite mad. Jinks burst out laughing at their astonished faces.

'Don't look so surprised,' he said. 'I am just going to play a very simple trick on the Enchanter, that's all, and you must be my servants and help me.'

'We'll do our best,' said Feefo.

How the Great Enchanter was Captured

Leaving their car behind them, they set off up the hill to the palace, Feefo and Tuppeny holding up Jinks's cloak behind him for all the world as if he were very grand indeed.

Three heralds with silver trumpets stood at the gates of the palace, and when they saw the little procession coming they blew loud blasts on their trumpets in welcome. The glass door of the palace swung open in front of them and the three goblins marched inside.

What a strange sight met their wondering eyes! The ceiling of the palace hall was so high that it was lost in mist. Great glass pillars stood here and there, wreathed in strange, coloured flames that licked up and down the pillars all the time. The floor was black, so black that it seemed as if the goblins were walking on nothingness.

At the end of this hall was a high platform and on it a great glittering throne. Here sat Know-All, the Enchanter, King of Topsy-Turvy Land, but not at all topsy-turvy himself. His eyes were as sharp as needles, and his mouth was so thin that it looked like a thread of cotton.

'Here comes Minky-Monk, the Mighty Magician!' yelled Tuppeny, in his enormous voice. Jinks bowed deeply to the Enchanter, who nodded his head.

'Why do you come to me?' he asked, and his strange voice seemed to come from a hundred years away.

'I come to test your powers!' said Minky-Monk, boldly. 'I am a clever magician, some say even cleverer than you, and I have come to see what wonderful things you can do.'

'First show me what *you* can do!' said Know-All.

'Well, to begin with, I can easily do the three things I read on your proclamation,' said Jinks.

'Impossible!' said Know-All. 'No one can raise dust from the magic black stone in my palace garden – it is as hard as iron. And certainly none can show me anything never seen before, for I have lived a thousand years and in that time I have seen all there is to be seen,

and known all there is to be known. As for reading my thoughts, such a thing could never be done, for they are as secret as a cat's footfall!'

'I will strike dust from your black rock!' cried Jinks. 'Come, let us go to it!'

The Enchanter arose and went down the long, misty hall to the glass door. It swung open and he and the goblins passed outside. A vast black rock, whose surface was as smooth as iron, stood within a grove of trees.

'There is the rock,' said Know-All. 'Stand upon it, Magician, and see how vain are your words!'

'Allow me to change my soft slippers for my shoes,' said Jinks, and slipped on his shoes carefully under his green cloak. Then he stepped on to the rock.

'Onnatipparootipoonaroryma!' he shouted, pretending that he was making a magic spell. He began to dance and jump about on the rock, and to the Enchanter's enormous surprise black dust flew out!

Tuppeny and Jinks turned away to hide their smiles. They knew it was only the soot in Jinks's shoes – but the Enchanter didn't! No, he stood there, with his mouth half open in wonder, and Jinks took the chance of kicking a cloud of soot towards him. Know-All shut his mouth with a snap, and began to cough and sneeze.

Jinks jumped and bounded, kicked and stamped all the harder till the air around was completely full of black dust, and Tuppeny and Feefo were coughing too.

'Enough, enough!' cried the Enchanter at last, seeing his hands and clothes getting black and dirty. 'I see you are very strong, Minky-Monk, and there is no doubt that you have kicked black dust from my magic rock.'

Jinks jumped down from the rock, very hot, and panted like a race-horse. They all returned to the palace and three servants took the goblins to three great bathrooms, where they bathed themselves and cleaned away the sticky soot.

Then back to the strange hall they went, staring in amazement at the flames that licked the glass pillars from top to bottom. The Enchanter was sitting on his throne, and as he was now quite clean the goblins thought he must have had a bath too!

'And now show me something that no one has ever seen before!' said Know-All.

'That's easy!' said Jinks, and he carefully took the brown egg out of his pocket. Know-All stared in amazement when he saw a hen's egg held out to him.

'Do you say that no one has ever seen that egg before?' he cried, scornfully. 'The hen has seen it – you have seen it – '

'Wait,' said Jinks. He suddenly crashed the egg on to the floor. It broke, and the yellow yolk streamed out.

'Tell me,' said Jinks, grinning. 'Has anyone in the world ever seen that yolk before, oh Enchanter?'

Know-All stared at it in anger. No, no one had ever seen that before, of course! It had been close-hidden in the shell, it could not be seen unless the egg was broken.

'This is but a trick,' said the Enchanter, harshly.

'No trick, but truth,' said Jinks, bowing.

Know-All sat silent for a moment. Then he spoke again, in his far-away voice.

'And now, oh very clever magician, tell me what I am thinking!'

Jinks stepped forward and looked into his deep eyes. 'You are thinking,' he said, 'you are thinking, oh Know-All, that I am Minky-Monk the Great Magician – but I am NOT! I am

Jinks, a sharp-witted goblin who is cleverer than you!'

Jinks threw off his green cloak and hat and stood before Know-All in his green suit and yellow stockings looking just what he was – a cheeky little green goblin.

The Enchanter leapt to his feet in surprise and rage. Thunder rolled through the palace and the flames that wreathed the pillars shot up higher than ever and changed to an angry red. Tuppeny and Feefo trembled, but Jinks stood unafraid.

For a moment the Enchanter seemed about to strike Jinks, to turn him into a beetle, to sweep him away to the moon, to do any one of the mighty things he was able to do. And then, very suddenly, seeing the goblin smiling there in front of him, he laughed.

'What's the use of being angry with a manni-kin like you!' he said. 'Yes, you are smart, you are sharp-witted, and I would dearly like to have you for my servant, though I should be afraid of you stealing my magic. But now, tremble, little goblin, for I will show you magi-cal things, things that will make you shiver and wish you had never come here to try your silly little tricks on me!'

'Great Enchanter, I ask for nothing better,'

cried Jinks, in a delighted voice. 'I have seen many great magicians and wizards perform their magic tricks, and if you can do better than they can, then indeed you will be clever. But I doubt it!'

The Enchanter took a thin silver stick and made three circles in the air, muttering as he did so. To the goblins' great astonishment he began to change! He grew an enormous spiked tail of a bright copper colour. His hands and feet changed to paws set with hundreds of claws – and then, before them was suddenly a giant dragon, almost filling the great hall, bellowing and roaring, sending flames and smoke out of his mouth!

'J-j-j-jumping b-b-beetles!' whispered Tuppeny, hiding under a chair. Feefo joined him – but Jinks stood watching the dragon, half afraid he was going to be eaten, but not daring to show his fear. The dragon suddenly dissolved into mist and out of it appeared the Enchanter again.

'What do you think of that?' he asked, proudly.

'Fairly good,' said Jinks. 'Not such a fierce dragon as I once saw the Green-eyed Witch change into, but still, not bad.'

The Enchanter went red with rage. He took up his silver stick again and waved it round

him. Immediately there appeared from the floor thousands of beautiful flowers growing and blossoming, sending out a very sweet scent. Jinks and the others gazed in delight. This was wonderful magic.

'Good,' said Jinks, at last. 'Quite good. I have never seen that done before in quite the same way.'

The garden vanished. The Enchanter glared at Jinks. He badly wanted to make him really astonished. He did not guess that the goblin was amazed already.

'You seem to think that everything I do is just ordinary,' he grumbled. 'Tell me something you would like me to do, and I will do it, no matter what it is! I will bring the moon down to the earth, fetch you a star, bring you the sea to my palace – only say what you wish, and I will do it.'

'Oh, don't do any of those things,' said Jinks, in alarm. 'I have found that it is the little, simple things that most wizards and enchanters cannot do.'

'Tell me one!' said the Enchanter.

'Well,' said Jinks, pretending to think hard, 'there is one thing that no one has ever shown me they can do yet – and that is, they can't turn themselves into a simple thing like a lump of sugar!'

'Easy!' shouted the Enchanter, scornfully. He picked up his silver stick and drew seven circles, each one smaller than the last, around him on the platform. Then he began to shrink very fast and to turn white. In two minutes' time there was a little white square thing in the middle of the smallest circle – a lump of white sugar.

Jinks, red with excitement, took a matchbox out of his pocket, emptied the matches on to the floor, made a dart at the piece of sugar, picked it up – and popped it into his match-box. He closed it quickly, and tied a piece of strong twine round and round it.

'Got him,' he said to the others, who were gaping at him in amazement.

'What do you mean, *got* him?' said Feefo.

'Well, haven't I got old Know-A-Lot as safe as can be?' said Jinks, doing a dance of joy. 'Isn't he in my match-box? He can't possibly get out, or make himself big because the match-box is very small and is tightly tied up. I can put him in my pocket and take him back to the King and Queen now!'

'Oh, Jinks, oh, Jinks, how clever, how wonderful you are!' cried Tuppeny and Feefo in joy.

The lump of sugar began to rattle about in the box and a high voice called out, 'What have you done to me? Open the box at once and let me go back to my own shape, or I will turn you into a spotted frog!'

'You just try!' said Jinks, cheerfully. 'If you get up to any tricks, Enchanter, I shall pop you into some warm water and let you melt away and that will be the end of you!'

'Come on,' said Tuppeny, pulling at Jinks's sleeve. 'Let's go. I don't much like this palace. Look at the flames on those pillars. They seem as if they are trying to put out hot tongues to reach us.'

Jinks took a look and then quickly ran out of the palace. No sooner had the goblins gone outside than there came a rumbling sound, and the whole palace went up in green flames! Nothing was left of it – not even a chair.

'That was a narrow escape,' said Jinks,

looking pale. 'Come on, let's get to our car.'

They ran to their car, jumped into it and set off hurriedly through the Land of Topsy-Turvy, not stopping for anything or anyone, not even for a policeman who wore a helmet on his feet and shouted strange, angry things to them.

They came to the Grumbling Wood and went through it as quickly as they could, and at last through the Land of Night. They were very glad when they saw the pretty toadstool houses of the Pixie-Folk.

Tiptoe was standing at their gate, watching for them. She waved in delight when she saw them coming up the lane.

'But where's the Enchanter?' she said, in disappointment, when she saw there was no one with them.

'Here!' said Jinks, and rattled his match-box.

'Whatever do you mean?' said Tiptoe. 'Let me see.'

'Oh, no!' said Jinks. 'If I let him out I really don't know *what* would happen. I'm just going off to the King and Queen to give him to them.'

The three jumped into their car and drove at top speed to the King's palace. They were shown into the King's presence at once, and the Queen came hurrying in when she heard the three goblins were there.

'Success, Your Majesties!' said Jinks, bowing low, and presenting the match-box to the King. 'Inside is a lump of white sugar – the Enchanter. If you want to get rid of him, put him into warm water and let him melt away.'

'Ow-ooh-ah!' yelled the Enchanter in the match-box, almost beside himself with fear and rage. 'Set me free, oh King, and I will do anything you please.'

'Don't listen to him,' said Jinks, earnestly. 'Make him do all you want, Your Majesty, and then decide what you will do with him.

The King and Queen were delighted and truly amazed. They listened to Jinks's story of the capture in admiration and praised the clever goblin highly.

'You shall have that palace over there, if you like,' said the King, and the goblins, looking out of the window, saw a fine palace glittering in the sunshine.

'Thank you,' said Jinks, bowing again. 'Do tell me what you are going to do about the Enchanter.'

'First he will have to bring back all the fairies

and elves he has spirited away,' said the King. 'Then he will have to put right all the harm and wrong he has done. Then, if he is still bent on wickedness, we shall melt him away – but if not, we may give him another chance.'

'Good, Your Majesty!' said Jinks. 'Now, if we may, we will leave you and go home.'

'Goodbye and very many thanks,' said the King, putting the match-box into his pocket. 'Take the palace whenever you like.'

Off went the goblins, talking at top speed. A palace of their own! Ooh!

'But, you know,' said Feefo, sensibly, 'a palace costs a great deal to run, what with servants and all that sort of thing. I think we had better let it to a prince or someone like that till we've enough money ourselves.'

'Oh, yes!' said Tuppeny, delighted. 'You know, Jinks, I do love our little cottage so much. I'm sure I should be homesick if we lived in the palace. Let's wait till we're very, very rich.'

Then off they went back to Hollyhock Cottage, anxious to tell Tiptoe about their palace – but, dear me, *how* pleased she was to hear that they were still going to live next door to her, after all!

The Adventure of the Surprising Blue Tablecloth

One day, when the goblins were out to tea with Tiptoe, and eating a lovely new chocolate cake made that morning, there came a knock at her door. Tiptoe went to answer it and gave a cry of surprise.

'Uncle Hoppetty! How nice to see you! Do come and have tea. There's a nice new chocolate cake.'

'Who are all these people?' asked Uncle Hoppetty, looking round at the three goblins, who had at once got up and bowed politely to the twinkling-eyed old man. He wasn't much bigger than they were, but he was very broad. His eyes were very blue and twinkled like stars on a frosty night.

'These are my great friends, Tuppeny, Jinks, and Feefo,' said Tiptoe. 'You must have heard of them, Uncle Hoppetty. They have just been clever enough to capture the great Enchanter Know-All for their Majesties, the King and Queen.'

'Bewhisker me! Is that really so!' said Tiptoe's uncle in surprise and admiration. 'Pleased to meet you, young men! Dear, dear, to think of meeting you here! Do tell me some of your adventures!'

So the three goblins took it in turn to tell all they had done, and Uncle Hoppetty listened in astonishment. Suddenly he banged his fist on the table, and cried:

'Bewhisker me! Have you ever heard of the Wonderful Tablecloth owned by Nobbly the Gnome? You really ought to go and get it!'

'Tell us about it,' begged Jinks.

'Well, this Tablecloth, which is as blue as the sky, is very magic,' said Hoppetty. 'No sooner do you spread it on a table and say 'Cloth, give me breakfast,' or 'Cloth, give me dinner,' than it at once covers itself with the most delicious dishes of all kinds for you to eat. I expect you have heard tales of it before. It was lost for many years and then Nobbly found it somewhere.'

'But wouldn't we have to pay a lot for it?' asked Feefo, doubtfully.

'That's just what I was coming to,' said
Uncle Hoppetty, his bright eyes shining. 'I
happen to know that Nobbly's house is falling
down and he doesn't want to build another one.
He has always longed to live in a palace – so,
as you don't want to live in *your* palace just yet,
why don't you go to Nobbly and offer him your
palace in exchange for his Tablecloth? I've no
doubt he is tired of it by now.'

'I say!' said Jinks, rubbing his hands

together in delight. 'Wouldn't it be fine to have a cloth like that? No more cooking! No more marketing! Ooh!'

'We'd ask you to tea every Friday,' said Tuppeny to Uncle Hoppetty.

'Bewhisker me! That's a fine idea!' said Hoppetty at once. He really did love a good meal.

'We'll do it!' said Feefo, making a noise like ten cats, purring for joy.

Uncle Hoppety looked round the kitchen in astonishment. 'Where's that cat?' he said to Tiptoe. 'I didn't know you had one.'

'There it is!' said Tiptoe, pointing to the grinning Feefo. 'Stop purring, Feefo, and pass the biscuits.'

It was soon settled that the very next day the goblins should set off to the Nobbly Gnome's and offer him the loan of their palace for his wonderful Tablecloth. The gnome didn't live very far away – only about eight hours' drive in the little green car – so if they started off in the morning, they could spend the night somewhere on the way back and arrive home the day after.

They cleaned up their car and Tiptoe packed sandwiches for them, and what was left of the chocolate cake. They set off at seven o'clock in the morning, when the silvery mist hung over the fields, and everything was very beautiful. Tiptoe wished she were coming with them, it was such a lovely day.

'Good-bye, good-bye!' she cried. 'Take care of yourselves, goblins, and come back safely with the Blue Tablecloth.'

'Of course!' shouted all three together, and then Feefo made a noise like fifty hooters honking, which made Jinks jump so much that he nearly drove the car into the hedge.

'Don't do that!' he said, fiercely. 'Or else, if you do, just warn me first.'

They drove on through villages and countrysides, through big goblin-towns, full of all kinds and colours of goblins, shouting, buying, selling. Some of them knew the three green goblins, but Jinks didn't stop.

They had their sandwich lunch in a little sunny dell by the side of a lane, and drank from a clear, bubbling brook near by. Then they packed themselves into the car again and once more set off for the Nobbly Gnome's.

They came to his town at last, and asked for his house. It was a large one, painted bright yellow, and it was certainly falling to bits.

One of the chimneys had gone, and part of the roof had fallen in, so that the rain fell through and wetted everything.

The goblins got out of their car and went to the door. The bell was broken and there was no knocker, so they had to rap with their fists.

'Come in, come in, come in!' shouted a voice, and Jinks pushed open the door. The goblins went inside and found themselves in a room, perfectly round, with a big fire burning in the middle. The Nobbly Gnome was sitting over it, reading a large book. He wore four pairs of spectacles on his nose and two on his forehead, so he really looked very funny.

'What do you want?' he asked, looking over the top of his four pairs of spectacles in rather a cross way.

'We've come to see if you'd like to live in a palace on a hill that belongs to us,' said Jinks. 'Your house seems to be falling down. It might fall on your head one day and that would be the end of you.'

'Stars and moon, do you really think it might?' cried the startled gnome, looking up at the ceiling nervously. 'Well, I've always wanted to live in a palace, and I'm sure it's very kind of you to offer me yours. I suppose you want something in return?'

'Well, we do rather,' said Jinks. 'We heard

you had a wonderful cloth that could bring any meal you wished for. Could you spare us that cloth, do you think, in exchange for the loan of our palace?'

'Certainly!' said the Nobbly Gnome, shutting up his book and sliding the two odd pairs of spectacles down on to his nose with the others. 'I'm tired of the cloth, you know. I've had it for about seventy years and I know all the breakfasts, dinners, teas and suppers it's got. I'll give it to you with the greatest pleasure, if you'll be kind enough to lend me your palace. Do you know if there is hot and cold water in all the bedrooms of your palace?'

'Sure to be,' said Jinks. 'It's quite a new one. You can wash yourself in every room if you like.'

'That really will be exciting,' beamed the gnome, who certainly looked as if he could do with a wash in some sort of basin. 'I have to pump my own water here, and as I always forget I can hardly ever wash.'

'No wonder you look a bit dir – ' began Tuppeny, but Feefo nudged him hard and he just stopped in time.

'Don't annoy him!' whispered Feefo. 'Nobody likes being called dirty.'

'Have you got the Tablecloth handy?' asked Jinks.

'Well – not exactly handy,' said the Nobbly Gnome, pushing all his spectacles back on to his forehead and looking round the kitchen. 'Let me see now. You might look in that cupboard over there. I believe I put it there when I filled the kitchen drawer full of mousetraps. My larder was full of mice, you know, and I really had to get some traps.'

'Did you catch many mice?' asked Jinks, politely, as he went to the cupboard.

'Well, no,' said the Nobbly Gnome. 'I forgot to set the traps, really, but I'm sure I should have caught hundreds if I hadn't forgotten.'

'It's not in the cupboard,' said Jinks. 'The cupboard is simply full of bottles of vinegar.'

'Dear me, so that was where the vinegar went to!' said the Nobbly Gnome in surprise. 'You know, I had a tremendous lot of onions in my garden last year, and I bought all those bottles of vinegar to pickle them. I couldn't think where I'd put the vinegar, so the onions were all wasted. It was such a pity.'

The three goblins stared at the gnome in astonishment. What a forgetter he was!

'Well, do you know where you put the Magic Cloth after you took it out of the cupboard to make room for the vinegar bottles?' said Jinks.

'Let me see now – yes, you might look in

the wood-box under the sink,' said the gnome, thinking hard. 'I often stuff things there to put them out of the way.'

'I think you ought to have been more careful of such a wonderful thing as that Tablecloth,' said Feefo, and the gnome looked half ashamed of himself.

'I was very careful of it when it gave me my meals,' he said, 'but after that it was just a nuisance.'

Tuppeny found the wood-box under the sink and took off the lid. It was full of shirts and socks, but there was no Blue Tablecloth there!

'Bless me!' said the gnome, in surprise, 'so that's where last week's laundry went to! Of course, I remember now! The boy wanted the laundry basket back, so I emptied everything out of the wood-box and stuffed my clean shirts and socks there. Well, well, I can put on a clean pair of socks now.'

'Yes, but where did you put the *TABLE-CLOTH?*' shouted Jinks, feeling that he might lose his temper at any moment.

'Oh, bother that wretched Tablecloth!' said the gnome, frowning. 'Don't I *keep* remembering where it is?'

'No, you keep remembering where it *isn't!*' said Jinks, sharply. 'Now, think hard, Nobbly Gnome. Where did you put it after you had taken it out of the wood-box?'

'I put it – I put it – in that big green teapot up on the dresser,' said the Nobbly Gnome, polishing up all his pairs of spectacles in a vexed manner.

'In the *tea*pot!' said all the goblins, in surprise. 'But whatever for?'

'Well, you must put things somewhere, mustn't you?' said the gnome, in a grumpy voice. 'And I never do use that teapot. It's much too big. It would do nicely for a hippo-potamus.'

Feefo at once made a noise like a hippo and the Nobbly Gnome gave a shriek and disappeared under the sofa.

'Don't be silly, Feefo,' said Jinks in despair. 'If you frighten him, he'll never remember anything at all. Fancy snorting like a hippo at an important time like this!'

Feefo stopped at once and went to the dresser where a giant-size teapot stood. He took it down and looked into it.

'There's no Blue Tablecloth here!' he said, in disgust. 'It's full of pearls!'

'Just fancy that now!' said the Nobbly Gnome. 'I wondered where I had put all my cat's pearls.'

'Your cat's pearls!' said Jinks. 'What next!'

'Oh, haven't you heard about my cat?' asked the gnome, in surprise. 'He's a marvellous cat. When he purrs, big pearls drop out of his mouth. I used to collect them and make them into necklaces for my friends, then I got tired of it. I emptied the pearls out of their box into that teapot the other day. I remember quite clearly now.'

'And what did you do with the Tablecloth, when you took it out of the teapot to make room for the pearls?' asked Jinks, patiently, beginning to feel this must be a most annoying sort of dream.

'I really don't know,' said the gnome, helplessly, looking round. 'Oh, look – there it is, hanging up by the sink, under our noses all the time!'

'Where?' said all the goblins, excitedly, looking at the sink.

'Why, that cloth there,' said the gnome, pointing to a grey and dirty dishcloth hanging on a nail.

'That *dish*cloth!' said Jinks, in horror. 'Do you mean to say you used that Magic Tablecloth for a *dish*cloth, Nobbly Gnome? How *could* you do such a thing?'

'Well, I must have *some*thing for a dishcloth, mustn't I?' grumbled the gnome. '*I* don't know where all my dishcloths have gone to. I had dozens.'

'They are probably in the dustbin, I should think,' said Jinks, going over to get the dirty cloth. He took some soap, pumped some water into a bowl and began to wash the cloth. It came a beautiful blue colour when it was clean. Jinks shook it out – and Tuppeny gave a shriek.

'Jinks! There's only half of it! Look!'

Sure enough it had been torn in half. You could see the ragged edge plainly.

'Is it any good when it is torn in half?' asked Jinks.

'Oh, no, none,' said the Nobbly Gnome, cheerfully. 'Yes, I remember tearing it in half now. I wanted the other piece to clean my boots with.'

Jinks groaned. He had certainly only just come to the rescue of the Tablecloth in time! It was Tuppeny who found the boot-box – and inside, for a wonder, was the other half of the Blue Tablecloth. It took a very long time to get it clean, for it was covered with black polish.

When both halves were clean and dry, Jinks hunted for a needle and cotton. There didn't seem to be such a thing in the Nobbly Gnome's house.

'And if there is, it won't be in the work-basket,' said Jinks. 'It will be in the kettle or somewhere like that!'

In the end Jinks opened his basket and from his tray took a reel of cotton and a packet of needles. Then he neatly sewed the two halves of the cloth together. It was mended!

'Now let's see it work!' said Tuppeny, excited.

The Nobbly Gnome took it and spread it smoothly on his table.

311

'Cloth, give us a good, late tea!' he commanded.

Wonder of wonders! Marvels of marvels! On to that bright blue cloth appeared two new loaves of crusty bread, a big dish of golden butter, a great jar of golden honey, one big fruit cake, a large dish of sardines in oil, a flat dish of delicious ham, a cold chicken and a steaming pot of sweet cocoa. Think of that!

'Ooh! This is the only sensible thing you've done so far!' said Tuppeny, hungrily, slapping the Nobbly Gnome on the back.

They all sat down and made an excellent

meal. It was half-past six and they were very hungry indeed.

'I'm sorry I can't ask you to stay here for the night,' said Nobbly, afterwards. 'But to tell you the truth, I've put my bed somewhere and I can't think where, so I only have a sofa to sleep on myself. But if you drive on for forty miles you'll come to an inn called "Welcome," and the landlord will be pleased to put you up, I'm sure.'

'Thank you,' said Jinks, getting up from the table. 'What do we do with all the remains of our tea?'

'Oh, just this,' said Nobbly, and he gave the cloth a tug. Immediately all the dishes disappeared, and the cloth was clean and bare. Nobbly folded it up, and gave it to Jinks, who put it safely into his biggest pocket.

'I suppose you wouldn't like to come with us, would you?' he asked the Gnome. 'We can't very well bring your palace to you, you see. You'll have to come and see it.'

'Oh, I'd love to!' cried Nobbly, joyfully. So they all packed themselves into the car, though it was a bit of a squeeze with four of them, and Jinks drove off through the night.

They arrived at the Welcome Inn at last and

Jinks hammered on the door, which was fast-shut.

'Who's there?' said a gruff voice, and a big head looked out of a window.

'Guests!' said Jinks. 'We want to stay the night.'

'I've no food for you and but one bed,' said the surly voice.

'Oh, never mind,' said Jinks, impatiently. 'We are tired. Let us in. Why do you call your inn "Welcome," if you greet your guests in this way?'

With a great deal of mumbling and grumbling the landlord came heavily down the stairs and unbolted the door. The goblins and the gnome stepped inside and shivered, for the inn was very cold and damp. They saw the glint of a fire in one room and went there.

'There's no food in the house, as I told you,' said the landlord.

'Don't worry, we've plenty for ourselves,' said Jinks, thinking of the Blue Tablecloth he had in his pocket.

'Is it out in your car then?' asked the landlord, seeing they had nothing with them. 'Shall I tell my servant to fetch it in for you?'

'No thanks, we've got it with us,' said Jinks, much to the landlord's amazement.

'There's a big bed in the next room,' said he. 'You can sleep there when you are ready. Good night to you.'

'Good night!' said everyone, and he went stumping out of the room.

The Black Cat and the Red Whip

'I don't like the landlord very much,' said Tuppeny.

'I've a good mind to make a noise like twenty more people arriving, and give him a fright,' chuckled Feefo.

'No, don't,' said Nobbly in alarm. 'He might turn us out and I'm *so* sleepy.'

'Anybody want a cup of hot milk and some biscuits before we go to bed?' asked Jinks, shaking out his wonderful Tablecloth and spreading it on the table.

'I'd like some milk and some chocolate biscuits,' cried Tuppeny at once.

'And I'll have some supper too!' said Feefo.

'Cloth, give us a light supper,' commanded Jinks. At once the cloth spread itself with a big jug of hot milk, two plates of sweet biscuits and a dish of small buns. All the goblins and the gnome helped themselves in delight – and not one of them saw the landlord peeping in amazement through the crack in the half-open door!

'So that's what they meant when they said they had their food with them!' he thought to himself. 'My, if I had that cloth, what fortunes I would make! I'd never need to go marketing, I'd never need to cook or bake. Everything I wanted I could get from that cloth.'

After a little while Jinks tugged the cloth and the remains of their supper vanished. He put it back into his pocket and they all four of them went into the next room. The bed was a big one, so they climbed into it and lay down comfortably in a row. Jinks was on the outside, Tuppeny and Feefo in the middle, and Nobbly by the wall, because he was so afraid of falling out.

Soon they were all asleep, tired out with their exciting day – and when little snores and snorts came from the bedroom, the big landlord crept through the door in his bare feet. The moon shone into the room and he saw that Jinks lay on the outside. That was lucky. He saw a corner of the Blue Tablecloth hanging out of the goblin's pocket and he gave it a gentle pull.

A little of it came out – then a little more. Jinks didn't stir. He always slept very soundly

indeed. The landlord pulled again – and in a few minutes' time he had managed to get the whole of the cloth into his hands.

318

He stole out of the room. He lighted a lamp and looked at the cloth. Had he got one like it in his linen chest?

He took the lamp and went to look. He pulled out white cloths, green ones, orange ones – and then two blue ones. One of them was a bright blue, almost like the Magic Cloth. The landlord tore it in half and neatly mended it again, just as he saw had been done to the Magic Cloth. Then he stole back to the bedroom and pushed his cloth gently into Jinks's pocket.

In the morning the three goblins and the gnome awoke and yawned. At first they wondered where they were, but very soon they remembered. They jumped out of bed, washed themselves out in the yard at the pump, and then went into the inn to pay the landlord and to have their breakfast.

Jinks shook out the cloth and spread it on a table. 'Cloth, give us a good breakfast,' he commanded. Everyone looked hungrily to see what sort of breakfast was going to appear. Eggs and bacon? Porridge and treacle? Kippers and toast?

The cloth lay there quite empty! Not a dish came, not a tiny piece of toast. Jinks stared in surprise. Then he spoke again. 'Come, come,

Cloth, give us a good breakfast and be quick about it!'

But no – the cloth wouldn't do a thing. It just behaved like an ordinary tablecloth and the goblins were most disappointed and amazed.

'Is it *my* cloth?' asked Nobbly, at last.

'Yes, look – here's the place where it was torn down the middle and I mended it,' said Jinks.

'I expect tearing it in half like that and using it for a dishcloth and a polishing rag has spoilt the magic,' said Feefo, gloomily. 'It just did a bit of magic yesterday, but I expect that's all it will do now. You ought to be ashamed of yourself, Nobbly Gnome, for using a wonderful thing like that in such wrong ways.'

'Shan't I get your palace now?' asked Nobbly, pushing all his spectacles up on to his head in despair.

'Of course not,' said Jinks. 'Unless you've anything else to give us in exchange that is as good as this cloth was.'

'Well – there's my cat,' said Nobbly. 'Would he do, do you think? He purrs pearls beautifully, you know.'

The three goblins cheered up at once. A cat that purred pearls would be almost better than a cloth that gave free meals!

'Yes, that would do,' said Jinks. 'Come on, let's drive back to your house, Nobbly, and get the cat.'

So back they went to Nobbly's house.

'Anyway, thank goodness the cat's alive and can't be put into all sorts of silly places like the cloth was,' said Feefo when they arrived.

'And can't be cut in half and used for a dishcloth,' said Tuppeny.

'Don't scold me so,' said Nobbly. 'If you do, I shall forget what the cat's name is and it will only come if it is called by its right name.'

'Jumping beetles!' groaned Tuppeny. 'Don't say you're going to forget the cat's name, Nobbly.'

'Well, I'm not quite sure, but I think it's something to do with a chimney,' said Nobbly, after thinking hard for a few minutes.

'Something to do with a chimney, Nobbly!' said Jinks. 'You must be mad.'

'A roof has to do with a chimney,' said Feefo. 'Perhaps the cat's name is Rufus.'

'Rufus, Rufus, Rufus!' shouted Jinks, at once. But no cat came.

'Perhaps it's a name *like* chimney,' said Tuppeny. 'Timmy or Bimmy, or something like that.'

321

So they tried Timmy and Bimmy, and Jimmy too, but no cat came at all.

'Try to think of its name again,' begged the goblin – but all Nobbly could say was that its name reminded him of chimneys.

'What's the cat like?' asked Tuppeny.

'Oh, as black as a sweep,' said Nobbly.

'Sweep, Sweep, Sweep!' called Tuppeny. No answer from any cat at all.

'Make a noise like cream being poured into a saucer, Feefo,' begged Jinks, suddenly. So Feefo pursed up his lips and made a thick, creamy, delicious sort of noise, which made everyone think of a jugful of cream being poured slowly into a saucer.

That did the trick! At once a large black cat came running in at the kitchen door, mewing loudly.

'Oh, look, here's Sooty!' shouted Nobbly in delight.

'Sooty! Is that his name?' said Jinks.

'Of course!' said Nobbly.

'Well, why couldn't you think of it before?' said Feefo. 'Making us waste all this time!'

'I always think of Sooty's name when I *see* him,' said Nobbly, 'but never when he isn't there. I just think of chimneys or something then.'

'Of course! Sooty chimneys!' said Jinks, with a groan. 'You've just got the most upside-down brains ever I knew, Nobbly. You'd be at home in Topsy-Turvy Land! It's a pity our palace isn't there.'

'Let's see the cat purr pearls,' said Feefo.

So Nobbly stroked the big cat, and when it began to purr, what a strange thing! Creamy

pearls fell from its mouth and rolled about the
floor. The goblins watched in delight.

They spent the day at Nobbly's, for he was
anxious to pack up some of his books to take
to the palace, and it took a long time to find
them. But at last they were all in the car and
the four of them set off again, the cat sitting
on Nobbly's shoulder.

'We'll have to spend the night at the same
inn,' said Jinks. 'And the landlord will have to
give us a meal this time, for our wonderful
cloth no longer works!'

The landlord was surprised to see them, but
he let them come in. They took the cat in with
them, and it sat silent by the fire.

'We haven't our food with us this time,' said
Jinks. 'You must get us some.' The landlord
said he would, and went away. He returned
with a good supper, and asked the goblins to
pay him.

'We haven't the money to pay you now,' said
Jinks, feeling in his pocket. 'Would you accept
a few pearls instead?'

'Certainly,' said the landlord, in surprise. He
made up his mind to watch where these strange
little visitors got their pearls from – and when
he saw them stroking the cat, which let pearls
fall from its mouth as it purred, he was more

astonished than when he had seen the wonderful cloth!

He glued his eye to the crack in the door, and marvelled. Could he steal that cat too? It should be easy enough!

When the goblins and the gnome were asleep, the landlord crept to the bedroom. The cat lay at the foot of the bed, awake. It was listening for mice.

'Mouse!' whispered the landlord. 'Mouse!'

At once Sooty jumped off the bed and ran to the door. The landlord popped him into a large bag he had ready and tiptoed away at once. He looked at the cat closely when he was in his room and saw that it was black all over except for a little piece under its chest, which was white.

'Just like my old stable cat!' he chuckled. 'I'll go and get her!'

Out he went and soon tempted the stable cat to come to him by dangling a herring behind him on a string. He caught her and took her to the goblins' bedroom. He shut her in there with them and went off to bed, delighted with his evening's work.

The next day, what a commotion when the goblins found that the cat wouldn't give them a single pearl! They stroked her gently, they

stroked her hard – she purred as loudly as she
could, surprised at all the attention she was
getting. But she was only an ordinary stable cat
and no matter how she purred, no pearls fell
from her whiskered mouth!

'I suppose your cat's no use away from
home,' said Jinks, at last. 'It's most disappointing, really. Now whatever are we to do?'

'Have you anything else magic?' asked
Feefo.

'Only a red whip,' said poor Nobbly. 'You
can have that if you like.'

So back to his house they went, and wonder

326

of wonders, they found the Red Whip almost at once! It actually stood in the right place – in the umbrella stand!

'What does it do?' asked Jinks, taking it out and looking at it.

'It just whips people who are my enemies,' said Nobbly. 'It isn't very magic, I'm afraid. If a burglar came in the night it would hop out of the umbrella-stand and whip him till he went away.'

'Well, it doesn't sound as if it would be much use to us,' said Jinks, doubtfully.

'Can't I have your palace then?' said poor disappointed Nobbly, his eyes filling with tears. Tuppeny was upset to see him unhappy and put his arms round him.

'Jinks, do let him have our palace,' he begged. 'After all, he was quite willing for us to have his Tablecloth and his Cat, and he couldn't help it if the magic went out of them.'

'All right,' said Jinks, at once. 'Cheer up, Nobbly Gnome. You can have our palace for a year at any rate. And if we manage to sell your Red Whip to anyone you can have the palace for longer.'

'Oh, thank you!' said Nobbly, quite cheered up. 'Well, shall we start off now?'

'We might as well,' said Jinks. 'We could

get to Heyho Village by this evening if we set off now. We don't need to stop at that horrid Welcome Inn again then.'

'Come on,' said Feefo, clucking like a hen for joy, and making Nobbly look everywhere to see where the chicken was. He never could get used to Feefo's noises.

'What about the cat?' said Tuppeny. 'It came back with us in the car. It's rather a nice cat and it's a shame to leave it here all by itself. It might starve. We'd better take it with us. It might suddenly get its magic back again. You never know!'

'Yes, let's take it,' said Jinks. 'Where did it go when it got out of the car?'

Nobody had noticed.

'And I've forgotten its name again,' said Nobbly in dismay.

'Well, *we* haven't!' said Feefo at once. 'Our brains aren't quite so muddled as yours, Nobbly. Now think – it's something to do with chimneys!'

But poor old Nobbly could *not* remember the name.

'You have a most wonderful forgettery!' said Feefo. 'Now, where's that cat? Sooty, Sooty, Sooty!'

No cat appeared.

'That's funny,' said Nobbly, puzzled. 'Sooty always comes when his name is called. Always!'

'SOOTY, SOOTY, SOOTY!' yelled Tuppeny in his most enormous voice, and startled Nobbly so much that he sat down suddenly in a basin of potatoes that he had stupidly left on a chair behind him.

'I wondered where I had left those potatoes,' he said, drying himself. Tuppeny shrieked with laughter, and Jinks and Feefo both thought that really Nobbly was quite mad.

'Where *is* that cat!' said Jinks, crossly. 'If we don't find it we shall never start off in time to get to Heyho Village today.'

But, you know, they didn't find the cat, and it wouldn't even answer when they called 'Sooty, Sooty!' Nor would it come even when Feefo made a noise like cream being poured out, again, which was really very extraordinary, Nobbly thought.

'Well, we can't wait any longer,' said Jinks.

'I'm awfully hungry,' said Tuppeny.

'So am I,' said Feefo. 'Hadn't we better have dinner before we start, Jinks?'

'All right,' said Jinks, sighing. 'But that means we shan't get home tonight. We shall have to stay at that horrid inn again.'

They found some sardines and bought some

bread and some butter. Jinks took some chocolate and apples out of his wonderful basket so they made quite a good meal. Then they all packed themselves into the car again and set off.

But it was an unlucky day for them. The little car got a bad puncture and it took Jinks a long time to get the wheel off and the spare wheel on. It was past tea-time before they could start again, and just as it was getting dark they drew up at the Welcome Inn.

The landlord gaped in surprise to see the little party again, and welcomed them more heartily than he had done before, for he felt sure that they would have something valuable that he might steal again.

'Bring us supper,' said Jinks, flinging his hat down on a table. 'We are hungry, so please be quick.'

'I say! We've left that Red Whip out in the car!' whispered Tuppeny to Jinks. Jinks went out at once to fetch it and brought it back. The landlord watched him and made up his mind that he would peep through the crack of the door and see what the whip did for the goblins and the gnome.

'Maybe it cracks out gold for them!' he thought to himself.

He took in a fine supper, which he had got from the Magic Tablecloth, and he was careful to lock up the black cat so that it would not go near his guests. Then he put his eye to the crack in the door to watch what the Red Whip did.

But to his great disappointment it did nothing at all! Jinks stood it by his chair whilst he ate his supper, and took no further notice of it.

'We'll go to bed now,' he said, when they had all finished. 'Then we can get up early in the morning and get to Heyho Village in good time. Tiptoe will be wondering whatever has become of us!'

So off they went to lie in the big bed. Jinks took the Red Whip with him and stood it at the head of the bed. The landlord watched him and felt perfectly certain that the Whip was magic in some way. He would steal it that very night! There was an old whip in the stables he could dip into a pot of red paint and put into its place.

So, when the goblins and the gnome lay fast asleep, the landlord crept once more into their bedroom. He tiptoed to the head of the bed and put out his hand for the Whip. But, strange to say, it dodged to one side!

'Oho!' said the landlord, pleased to find it was magic, just as he had thought. 'So you *are* magic, are you!'

He made another grab at it – and then the Whip did an even stranger thing. It gave a loud crack and struck the surprised landlord on the back.

'Ow!' he yelled, jumping three feet into the

air with fright and pain. The Whip gave another loud crack and hit the frightened man once more. He yelled in horror – and, of course, all the goblins and the gnome woke up in a hurry! Jinks lighted the lamp – and what a strange sight he saw!

The Whip was whipping the landlord all round the room! He ran out into the passage and the Whip followed him, whipping away for all it was worth! The landlord yelled and the Whip cracked so there was a fine old noise.

'Shall I stop the Whip?' said Nobbly, anxiously.

'No,' said Jinks, a curious look coming over his face. 'No. That landlord must have come into our room to steal something or the Whip wouldn't have attacked him. Let it go on whipping him and see what he says.'

The landlord rushed into their room, crying big tears. The Whip followed, slashing away at his broad shoulders.

'Mercy, mercy!' begged the landlord, falling on his knees. 'Mercy, kind sirs!'

'What were you doing in our room?' asked Jinks, sternly.

'Nothing, nothing!' wept the landlord. At this the Whip attacked him all the more and he yelled with pain.

333

'Confess everything and we will stop the Whip from beating you!' said Jinks.

'I will tell you all,' sobbed the landlord, now almost frightened out of his wits. 'It was I who took your cloth and put another in its place. It was I who stole your cat and gave you my stable cat instead. I came to steal your whip tonight, but it set upon me like this.'

The goblins and the gnome listened in the greatest amazement and disgust. So that was what had happened! No wonder the cloth and

334

the cat would not give out their magic any more!

'Get us the cloth and the cat at once,' said Jinks. The landlord got up and staggered off, the Whip dancing nimbly round him and getting in a few good cuts whenever it saw a chance. Ah, truly the thief of a landlord was getting his punishment now!

He came back with the cloth in one hand and the cat in another.

'Sooty, Sooty!' cried Feefo. The cat purred with delight and at once pearls fell from its mouth. Jinks took the cloth, spread it and commanded it to give them a meal. At once it became covered with delicious dishes of food. It was the Magic Tablecloth, there was no doubt about it.

'Make the Whip stop beating me,' begged the landlord. 'I have given you back all I stole.'

'Whip, stop your antics and go back to Jinks,' commanded Nobbly. The Whip at once jumped into Jinks's hand and stood there quietly.

'You have had a good punishment for your dishonesty,' said Jinks, severely. 'See that you treat your guests fairly and honestly in future, for if I ever hear that you have been dishonest again I will send my Whip to you at once.'

'I will never rob anyone again,' wept the scared landlord. 'Oh, forgive me, and take your Whip away when you go tomorrow.'

The next morning the goblins and the gnome packed the cat, the cloth and the whip into their car, called out a last warning to the frightened landlord, who could hardly walk that morning, he was so stiff with his beating, and set off for Heyho Village.

'At last!' said Jinks. 'I began to think we should never get home again!'

'I'm getting so excited about my palace,' said Nobbly, rubbing his hands together. 'If you like you can have all three of my magic things, Jinks. I think they would be safer with you than with me. I can always borrow them if I want them.

'Of course!' said Jinks. 'You may be sure *we* shan't use the cloth as a dishcloth or a polishing rag, Nobbly, and none of us will forget Sooty's name!'

Sooty purred and a dozen pearls trickled down Nobbly's neck, for the cat was sitting on his shoulder as usual.

'Ooh!' he said, wriggling. 'Don't do that, Sooty. It tickles me.'

How pleased Tiptoe was to see them all! She and Uncle Hoppetty were waiting anxiously for them, and when they saw all the magic things they had with them, how surprised and delighted they were! As for Nobbly he nearly fell over himself with delight when he saw his palace!

'It's grand, it's grand, it's grand!' he sang, going into all the bedrooms and turning on the taps.

'Just you remember to turn them off again!' called Jinks, when the goblins left the gnome. 'Or you'll find you've got a swimming-pool instead of a palace!'

Then off they went to Hollyhock Cottage, chuckling loudly whenever they thought of dear old Nobbly and his upside-down brains!

The Lost Princess and the Bewitched Tree

One morning, when Jinks and Feefo were eating a good breakfast given to them by the Magic Tablecloth and Tuppeny was giving the black cat some milk in a saucer, there came the sound of someone running quickly up the path to the front door. Then little hands knocked on the door and a voice cried 'Oh, quick, quick, help me!'

Jinks leapt up and rushed to the door. He opened it and there stood the prettiest little pixie girl you could imagine! Her hair was as black as a rook's wing, and as curly as a lamb's coat. Her eyes were the colour of brown brooks and her face was like a flower.

But she was crying bitterly! Jinks took her hands and pulled her indoors. 'What's the matter?' he asked.

'Oh, green goblin, my sister has been stolen away!' sobbed the pixie. 'I'm the Princess

338

Lightfoot and my sister is the Princess Light-heart. Oh, please, please do find her for me.'

'Tell me how she was stolen,' said Jinks.

'Well, we were out in the woods,' said Light-foot. 'Lightheart is good at climbing trees – so she thought she would climb a tall one, right to the very top. She climbed up and up, and I watched her – but oh dear, oh dear, when she reached the top, she disappeared!'

'Jumping beetles!' said Tuppeny in surprise. He couldn't take his eyes off the pretty little pixie. He couldn't bear to see her crying. He

339

felt he wanted to put his arms round her and love her.

'Don't cry!' said fat little Tuppeny, pushing forward. '*I'll* rescue your sister for you!'

Jinks and Feefo were surprised to hear these bold words from timid Tuppeny. 'But how will you find out where she's gone?' asked Feefo.

'I shall climb the same tree as the Princess Lightheart and then I shall know what happened to her,' said Tuppeny, boldly.

'You dear, brave creature!' cried Lightfoot, and flung her arms round Tuppeny, who blushed with delight.

'I'd do anything in the world for such a dear, pretty little pixie,' he thought – but he didn't like to say it out loud.

'Come on, then,' said Jinks. 'Now or never!'

They set off down the garden path. Tiptoe, who was shaking a mat at her front door, saw them going and called out to know where. They told her.

'Goodness!' she said. 'I've heard of that bewitched tree before. Be careful, now, Tuppeny, or you'll disappear and never come back.'

They said goodbye to Tiptoe and went on their way to the woods. When they got there they hunted for the tree and soon found it because Lightfoot had carefully put a stick at the roots.

'That's it!' she said. 'Lightheart climbed right up to the top – and then vanished. Oh dear, oh dear, oh dear!'

'Oh, please don't cry!' said Tuppeny, in distress. 'I'll soon get your sister back again.'

He began to climb the tree. The others watched him. He climbed steadily up to the top, holding on tightly to the branches, calling out bravely to the others below.

And then, when he was almost at the top, he vanished! Yes, he really did! One minute he was there and the next he just wasn't!

'Tuppeny, Tuppeny!' shouted Jinks. But there was no answer.

'That's just what happened to Lightheart!' sobbed the little pixie princess. 'Oh, Tuppeny, now you've gone too!'

Jinks took out his handkerchief and wiped her eyes. Feefo gave another look upwards and then began to climb the tree as swiftly as he could.

'Feefo! Don't be silly!' cried Jinks. 'You'll vanish too!'

And sure enough, he did! Just at the top of the tree he disappeared into thin air. Not a sign of him was to be seen or heard!

341

Poor Jinks! He didn't know what in the world to do! There he was alone at the foot of the tree with the weeping little Princess.

'I'll climb up *nearly* to the top and see if I can find out anything,' he said at last to Lightfoot. 'Don't be afraid, now, I shan't go *right* to the top and vanish.'

So up he went, and stopped before he was quite to the top – and then, dear me, what a strange thing, he felt he must go on, and he climbed a few more steps.

Lightfoot, who was anxiously watching, suddenly gave a shriek. 'Don't go any higher, Jinks!'

But it was too late – Jinks too had gone! Then Lightfoot burst into sobs again and tore away through the wood, hurrying back to the kind-looking little fairy she had seen next door to the goblins' shop.

'Oh, oh!' she wept, when Tiptoe had run out to see what was the matter. 'They've *all* climbed the tree, and they've *all* disappeared.'

'Now what's all this?' suddenly cried a voice, and who should it be but the Nobbly Gnome come to see the three goblins. When Tiptoe told him what had happened he looked very solemn.

'A bad business,' he said, shaking his nobbly head. 'We must find out where they've gone.'

'But how can we when they are quite quite gone?' said Tiptoe, in despair.

'*I* shall go and find out!' said Nobbly.

'But you'll only disappear too,' said Lightfoot, dolefully.

'I daresay I shall,' said Nobbly. 'But *I* shall tie a long, long string to my foot, and when I disappear you must let the string unravel till it stops. Then you'll know I've got somewhere. I'll find some way of sending a message down the string to tell you where I've got to and how to rescue us.'

'How clever of you, Nobbly,' said Tiptoe, beaming all over her face. 'That really *is* a good idea. I don't know why the goblins say your brains are upside-down. I think you're very clever.'

Nobbly bought a most enormous ball of string. Then he and Tiptoe and the pixie Princess set off one more to the woods. When they came to the tree Nobbly said goodbye and climbed upwards, the string dangling down from his foot as he went. Tiptoe held the ball in her hand and it unravelled as Nobbly climbed.

Well, of course, the Nobbly Gnome vanished just as suddenly and completely as the others did. The string began to run out of the ball very quickly as soon as he disappeared and Tiptoe had hard work to hold it. At last, just as the string was nearly all gone, it stopped pulling out of the ball. Wherever Nobbly was he had stopped!

'Goodness knows how the gnome is going to send us a message down the string,' said Tiptoe, anxiously. 'We'd better sit down here and wait, even if it takes us all day.'

So they sat down and waited. The string hung quite still down the tree. Not even the wind moved it. Tiptoe leaned against the tree unhappily, thinking of all her missing friends. Poor little Lightfoot laid her head down on Tiptoe's knee and fell asleep. Soon Tiptoe closed her eyes and fell asleep too.

She was awakened by feeling the string jerking a little. She sat up and grasped her end firmly in her hand. It felt almost as if something or someone was coming down the string. Perhaps it was a message coming!

She woke Lightfoot and the two waited eagerly – and whatever *do* think came down the string? Guess!

Why, the little white mouse that always lived in Jinks's basket! What a surprise for Tiptoe! How pleased she was to see it!

344

'Ooh! A mouse!' said Lightfoot, with a squeal.

'Yes, it's Jinks's mouse!' said Tiptoe, and she picked up the little creature. It opened its mouth and a screwed-up piece of paper dropped out! A message, a message!

Tiptoe opened the paper and read the message:

'The top of this tree reaches into the Land of Nowhere. We are all here, quite safe, in an enormous castle, prisoners and servants of the Wise Witch, Konfundle-Rimminy. Please go and fetch the Red Whip from behind the mangle in the kitchen and tie the end of it to my mouse's tail. He is quite strong enough to drag it up the string. Give it to him tonight, then he will not be seen coming back. Don't worry about us. I will see that everyone comes back safely. Tell Lightfoot that Tuppeny sends his love and says that he will bring her sister back himself. JINKS.'

Tiptoe and Lightfoot wept for joy when they read the note. Tiptoe popped the mouse into her pocket, tied the end of the string safely to a branch and took Lightfoot back to the goblins' shop.

'It's no good going back to the tree until night,' said Tiptoe. 'So I think we'd better have something to eat. Oh, here is the Red Whip, behind the mangle, just as Jinks said. We'll take it into my cottage next door and then we'll have a good meal.'

They soon sat down and ate heartily, for they were very hungry. Then Tiptoe borrowed the goblins' car and she and Lightfoot set off to the palace where the little pixie's father and mother were waiting anxiously for their daughters' return.

They soon knew everything. Tiptoe asked them to send a hundred good soldiers to the tree in the wood, in case their help should be needed that night, and the King and Queen of Pixieland promised faithfully.

When it was dark Tiptoe and Lightfoot went to the woods, guarded well by a hundred good soldiers. When they got to the bewitched tree Tiptoe took out the little white mouse from her pocket. She carefully tied the thin end of the whip-lash to its tail, and then set it on the string that ran up into the darkness of the tree.

The little creature disappeared, dragging the Red Whip behind it. Soon both it and the Whip had disappeared.

The mouse, as soon as it had reached the top

of the tree, felt itself dragged by magic into the Land of Nowhere. It rose in a strong wind for some way and then fell to the ground. It heard the clatter of the Whip as that fell too. The mouse sniffed about for the string that would guide it to the Witch's castle. Soon it found it and, keeping it between its paws, ran swiftly along until it reached the dark, forbidding castle, with its small, slit-like windows lighted here and there.

The mouse went in at a small hole under-

neath the walls. The Whip dragged behind it
and almost stuck. The mouse went back and
nibbled the hole a little larger. It was a very
intelligent creature, anxious to do its little best.

The Whip slipped through the hole. The
mouse ran into a big hall and made for the
stairway. Up the stairs it went, the Red Whip
dragging behind it. Nobody was about, for it
was in the middle of the night – but the mouse
was half-afraid at any moment that the sharp-
eared old witch would come popping out of a
door. But nothing happened at all.

Up and up the mouse went, and up and up.
At last it reached the very top of the castle. It
came to a great yellow door, thick and solid.
There was a small crack underneath and the
mouse crept under it. The Whip followed.
There was only just room for it.

Inside the room, which was perfectly round
and very bare, sat the three goblins, Nobbly the
gnome and a little pixie Princess, Lightheart, as
pretty as Lightfoot, but a little bigger. She had
been crying and Feefo had his arm round her,
comforting her.

'Here's the mouse!' cried Jinks, holding up
the candle as the mouse squeezed itself under
the door! 'Oh, and it's brought the Whip!
Good!'

The white mouse ran up to Jinks and he carefully untied the end of the whip-lash. He saw that the mouse's tail was red where the twine had rubbed it, so he took a little pot of ointment and smeared it on gently. The mouse squeaked gratefully and then ran up Jinks's leg and into the basket, where it sat down comfortably inside a roll of blue ribbon.

'Now!' said Jinks, looking round at the others. 'All we've got to do is to make a most enormous noise which will make the witch or her servants come to us, and then we will set the Whip on them – and if it acts like it did with the landlord of the Welcome Inn, my goodness, what a surprise our enemies will get! Be ready to escape as soon as there is a chance. Feefo, will you look after Princess Lightheart? Nobbly, you keep with Tuppeny. I will lead the way. Now then – everyone make as loud a noise as they can!'

At once a most fearful noise began! You should have heard it! Tuppeny roared at the top of his enormous voice. Lightheart squealed. Nobbly groaned in his deepest voice. Jinks shouted and yelled and stamped. And Feefo – well, Feefo did better than he had ever done before!

He thundered like three thunderstorms! He

roared like fifty dragons! He clanked like
twelve engines gone wrong. He buzzed like a
million bees! He jingled like a thousand bells!
He was magnificent.

It was no wonder that the Witch Konfondle-
Rimminy woke up from her sleep with a dreadful start and sat up in bed with all her hair
standing on end. It was not surprising that her
servants came howling in fright to her room,
begging her to save them from whatever it was
that was making such a terrible noise.

The witch listened. The noise was coming
from the topmost room of the topmost tower.
It was her prisoners! How dare they do that?
How dare they wake her up! Aha, oho,
grrrrrumph, wouldn't she just show them what
she thought of people who did things like that!

Up she jumped and threw on her black
cloak. She took her broomstick with her to beat
her prisoners and, followed by all her servants,
little black imps with bright green eyes, she
flew up the long, long stairs on her broomstick.

'Sh! Here she comes!' said Jinks, who was
listening at the door. 'Be quiet, now!'

Everyone was quiet. The witch fumbled for
her key, put it into the lock and turned it.
Then she unbolted the long bolts and threw
open the door, glaring angrily.

'Whip, do your work!' shouted Jinks, and threw the Red Whip straight at the witch. And then – jumping beetles! How that Whip enjoyed itself! How it slashed and cracked! How it jumped here and darted there, getting in a cut at this little black imp and a slash at that one! The witch yelled when she felt it coiling round her and fled down the stairs, followed by all her imps in a fearful panic.

'Come on, quickly!' said Jinks to the others.

351

Feefo put his arm round Lightheart and helped her down the stairs. Tuppeny took Nobbly's hand and ran with him – and it was a good thing he did for Nobbly was in such a state of excitement that he might easily have run backwards or round and round, instead of down the stairs!

The Whip cleared the way beautifully for them. No matter where the witch hid or what she did, that Whip found her out and punished her for all the wicked deeds she had ever done! The black imps fled into cupboards and under chairs, but it wasn't a bit of good, the Whip poked them out!

Outside the castle it was dark, and Jinks stopped. 'Wait,' he said, feeling about. 'I must find that string that runs from Nobbly's foot to the bewitched tree. It's too dark to find the way ourselves.'

Tuppeny found it at last, and slowly they all followed Jinks, who let the string run through his hands as he went forward. Feefo had tight hold of Lightheart, who thought he was the nicest, kindest person she had ever met. Tuppeny had hold of Nobbly.

'Shall we be all right now, Jinks?' asked the little Princess, still half-frightened.

'Yes, I think so,' said Jinks. 'There's only

one thing that is worrying me. The witch will soon find out how to get rid of that Whip, for she is very clever – and what will happen when she comes after us? She has a whole army of black imps, you know.'

'Well, we must just hurry up, that's all,' said Feefo. 'Don't be frightened, Lightheart, *I'll* look after you.'

For some time there was no sound behind the little company hurrying along in the dark, guided by the string. Then Feefo's sharp ears heard something! It was the pattering of hundreds of tiny feet – the black imps!

'They're coming!' he cried to the others. 'Hurry!'

How they hurried – but the pattering behind grew louder and louder, and Jinks felt sure the witch was coming too, riding on her big broomstick!

Suddenly Jinks's foot knocked against something and the string seemed to disappear downwards.

'Here's the tree!' he cried, thankfully. 'If only we can get down it quickly!'

Down they all climbed in the dark, Feefo half-carrying little Lightheart – and climbing behind them, squealing and squawking, came

hundreds of black imps, with the witch behind them!

But what a surprise! At the bottom of the tree was the big army of soldiers sent by the King and Queen of Pixieland! They drew their swords, which glinted in the light of many lanterns, and the black imps, terrified, swarmed back up the tree, crying 'We're afraid, we're afraid!'

'We'll cut down the tree before the old witch climbs down herself!' cried Jinks.

But no one had an axe! So Jinks quickly

354

opened his basket, and there, right in the front, was a sharp axe! Good!

He took it and at once began to chop the bewitched tree. The axe was sharp and Jinks was strong.

'Move away!' cried the goblin. 'The tree will fall!'

Everyone moved to a safe distance and watched. Suddenly Nobbly gave a shout and pointed up the tree.

'The witch is climbing down!'

So she was – but Jinks didn't stop his work. Chop – chop – chop – the axe bit deep into the tree and, just as the old witch Konfondle-Rimminy was half-way down the tree, down it came with a groan and a crash!

The witch fell too – and as she touched the ground she disappeared into smoke!

'That's the end of *her*!' cried Jinks. 'Now we're all right! Hurrah!'

'Look! The dawn is coming!' cried Nobbly, pointing to the east. Everyone stood and watched the sun rise, a big golden ball that lighted up the wood and made everything new and beautiful.

'We must take the Princesses back to their parents,' said the Captain of the soldiers. 'I expect the King and Queen of Pixieland will send for you to thank you and reward you for your great help some time during the day.'

'Goodbye, darling Feefo,' said Princess Lightheart, hugging Feefo.

'Goodbye, darling Tuppeny,' said Princess Lightfoot, and she hugged fat little Tuppeny, who was simply delighted.

The soldiers marched away with the Princesses, and the goblins, Nobbly and Fairy Tiptoe went back to Hollyhock Cottage, talking nineteen to the dozen all the way.

'It *was* good and brave and clever of you to come and rescue us like that,' said Jinks to Nobbly. 'I don't know what we'd have done without you and dear Tiptoe. We should never have escaped from that tower in the Land of Nowhere!'

'We'd better all have a little sleep before we do anything,' said Tiptoe, yawning. 'If you've got to go to the Court of the King of Pixieland, goblins, you'll have to look your smartest, too, you know. I expect you'll get a fine reward.'

'Well, you and Nobbly shall share it all!' said Jinks. 'You are the best friends anyone could have!'

Soon all of them were fast asleep. They were awakened by loud knocking on the door – messengers from the King of Pixieland begging the three goblins, the gnome and the Fairy Tiptoe to attend at the Court at three o'clock that afternoon.

'Jumping beetles!' said Tuppeny, excited. 'What adventurous lives we lead nowadays! Where's my best suit?'

They spent the rest of the morning getting ready. How grand they all were, to be sure! In brand-new green and yellow suits, with yellow feathers in their jaunty green hats, the goblins were a sight to see. Nobbly had really washed himself well for once, and wore a red tunic with green stockings, and a funny round cap with little feathers sticking up all round the rim.

Tiptoe looked the loveliest of them all. She had on a new frock made of cornflowers and she wore a blue fillet round her lovely hair. Jinks looked and looked at her. She was prettier than a princess, really!

They all packed themselves into the little green car and drove off to the palace. Six heralds with long golden trumpets were awaiting them and sounded a fine fanfare as the car drew up at the gates. Footmen dressed in blue and silver took them into the palace, which, although it was not nearly so grand as the King of Fairyland's palace, was really very beautiful.

The King and Queen were sitting on their thrones, wearing their crowns. Beside them, one on each side, sat the Princesses Lightfoot and Lightheart, looking very lovely in their crowns and long red cloaks.

The three goblins and the gnome went up and bowed low to Their Majesties. Tiptoe was shy and hung back, but Princess Lightfoot jumped up and drew her down beside her.

'We are very grateful to you all for rescuing our Princess Lightheart from the Land of Nowhere,' said the King. 'We wish to thank you and reward you. Ask what you please and

you shall have it. What do you wish? A palace?
Gold? Precious stones?'

'I don't really think there's anything I want,
thank you, Your Majesty,' said Jinks. 'I am
very happy as I am.'

'Well,' said Tuppeny, blushing a bright red,
'there's only one thing *I* want, Your Majesty.'

'What is that?' asked the King, kindly.

'Well – you see – it's like this – ' stammered
Tuppeny. 'I'd like – very much like – to marry
that dear little Princess Lightfoot – if she'd
have me, that is.'

'Oooooh!' squealed Lightfoot in delight and
she rushed at Tuppeny and hugged him. 'Oh,
Father, may I? He's so kind and brave and
jolly.'

'And *I'd* like to marry Lightheart!' said
Feefo, boldly. 'That's the only reward *I* want.'

'But, bless us all, you haven't even got a
palace, or a present to offer my daughters!'
cried the King.

'Oh, yes, we've a fine palace,' said Feefo, at
once. 'The King of Fairyland gave it to us for
something we did for him. And as for a present
– here is a pearl necklace made of the famous
pearls our black cat drops from its mouth when
it purrs!'

At the same moment Tuppeny took a pearl

necklace from his pocket, and Feefo took one from his and they both knelt down in front of the Princesses and offered the lovely, gleaming beads to them.

'Well, if Lightfoot and Lightheart wish to marry you, then that shall be your reward,' said the King at last. 'You seem to be brave and good little goblins. Come back tomorrow and we will have the wedding. Then you can all go off to your palace and live happily ever afterwards!'

'Oh, thank you, Your Majesty!' said Feefo and Tuppeny, delighted. They bowed, kissed the Princesses goodbye and went backwards out of the King's presence, red with excitement and delight. Nobbly, Feefo and Tiptoe followed.

Jinks said nothing at all as they drove home. He looked very miserable.

'What's the matter?' asked Tuppeny, when they were all having a good tea at Hollyhock Cottage.

'Matter enough,' said Jinks. 'What am I going to do without you two? Will Nobbly come to live with me?'

'Oh no,' said Nobbly, at once. 'I love living in a palace and it will be such fun having the two Princesses and Tuppeny and Feefo there too.'

'I shall be very lonely,' said Jinks, sadly. Then he felt a little hand slipped into his and saw Tiptoe's sweet face smiling at him.

'Why need you be lonely?' she said. 'Don't you like me? Couldn't *we* get married too and go and live at the palace as well?'

'Oh Tiptoe, of course!' cried everyone in delight. 'Why ever didn't we think of it before! Of course you must marry Jinks and come and live at the palace too! What fun! And we'll keep this little cottage for ourselves, so that sometimes we can come back here and remember the fine times we have had together.'

'What about Nobbly?' asked Jinks. 'There's no one for *him* to marry.'

'*That* doesn't matter,' said Tuppeny. 'What good would a wife be to Nobbly? He'd forget all about her, and shut her up in the dog-kennel or something.'

'Yes, I should,' said Nobbly, sighing. 'I shall be quite happy just living with you all. It will be so nice to have meals all together!'

Well, the next day they were all married, and the wedding was the grandest one held for a hundred years. Bells rang, trumpets sounded,

people cheered, and everything was as merry as could be.

Then the three goblins took their pretty little wives and rode with them in a grand coach to their palace, Nobbly followed behind driving the little green car. All the people cheered as they passed.

'Hail to Prince Jinks and his wife Fairy Tiptoe! Hail to Prince Feefo and the Princess Lightheart! Hail to Prince Tuppeny and the Princess Lightfoot!'

'Jumping beetles!' said Tuppeny, happily. 'Listen to that! We're princes now!'

362

'You deserve it!' shouted Nobbly, behind them. 'Three cheers for us all!'

And now they are all *very* busy indeed, trying to live happily ever after.